Amidst the noise, fumes, soot and chaos of New York's West 22nd Street, some tiny green living thing is somehow poking, pushing its way up through the crack of grimy pavement. Unaware passersby might trample it, but Hannibal Xavier Serendipity would notice and care.

THE STREET KIDS

Written and Illustrated by
|HERBERT DANSKA|

Alfred A. Knopf   *New York*

·THE STREET KIDS·

This title was originally catalogued by the Library of Congress as follows:

Danska, Herbert.
 The street kids. written and illustrated by Herbert
Danska. New York. Knopf [1970]

  160 p. illus. 24 cm.

  Mr. Serendipity and an eighty-six-year-old friend finds a way to
bridge the generation gap after children taunt them at a strike-
bound construction site.

  [1. Strikes and lockouts—Fiction] I. Title.

PZ7.D238St   [Fic]   70–84568
ISBN 0–394–90495–8   MARC
Library of Congress   71 [4]   A C

This is a Borzoi Book published by Alfred A. Knopf, Inc.

To my wife Dolores, with love.

CONTENTS

THE STREET KIDS

·CONDEMNED·

X: Marked for demolition.

Rooted to a worn place on the linoleum, old Serendipity blinked up at his front window. The appearance outside it of a luminous green banshee leering in at him would have sent fewer shudders flopping from his spine into the pit of his stomach. He tried to say something, but managed only to click his false teeth.

Suddenly the old man felt very old. As if the world were crumbling down about him—that is, his world—snug and secure for so many years beneath the twin-tenements. He felt as if nothing in his parlor, not even his treasured books, belonged to him now, nor he, to any of it. In the endless moment

even the bumps in the basement walls seemed unfriendly. Old Serendipity the janitor stood feeling like a stranger, an unwelcome stranger, in his own home.

Finally, in a voice as dingy as the light he wailed, "Oh, me. They're . . . here." There could be *no* doubt of this.

Surely he had known it was coming. Months ago, he had gotten a notice in his mailbox along with the twenty-four tenants upstairs. He had known, but could never quite bring himself to accept the typewritten words as fact—as real. It had been one thing to read it in a cold formal letter, and another to see it. Right here, before him, staring him in the face . . .

The janitor's eyes flickered across the room for an instant to see Ag perched shakily on top of a bookcase, then returned forward just as the workman in the cellar archway outside showed up at another parlor window.

There, old Serendipity watched it happen once more. The gloved hand with the dripping brush painted a second X. From corner to corner . . . across the grimy windowpane, frames and all . . . a broad, wet, and very white X.

The pair of white Xs filled the room with their ominous, silent presence. It was like having a sentence of exile passed on him by some faceless judge, somewhere. For a split second the old man saw himself and Agamemnon wandering homeless through New York—through the streets of the monster city overhead.

The painter outside was now gone. Old Serendipity plucked nervously at his beard then blew his nose. Clearing his throat, he tried to hide the shock he felt from his friend, to sound casual.

"Say," he began weakly, "how'd you get yourself up there, Ag?" His forced smile quivered as he studied the look Agamemnon shot back at him from the shadows over the bookcase.

It was almost an accusing look, one the old janitor knew very well.

By jumping, old man, jumping! How else?

"Mm, yes, of course," the man mumbled sheepishly, hitching up his stained and baggy workpants.

He should have known better to ask Agamemnon such a foolish question. Clearly his goat was jumpy and crankier than his usual cranky self. The day had begun badly; the old man had sensed this since dawn. And on the eve of his birthday, too. The janitor wagged his head. How much, he wondered, did Ag know about what was going on? Those two large shiny eyes kept staring down at him.

For lack of anything better, Mr. Serendipity said, "Saw that tom pal of yours prowling the back alley, looking for you, I bet he was. Nice morning . . . er, why don't you stroll out and see if you can fin—"

Now what, old man?

"How's that?" the old man said fuzzily, pretending to himself he didn't know what his goat was getting at.

What do you do now, old man? That is, what do we do now? Huh?

"Oh." Mr. Serendipity fell silent, trying to think fast. So he knows. Doesn't he always? Can't keep anything from him, can I?

The janitor stepped forward and reached up to pat Ag's

flank to soothe him, only to see his goat shrink back from his touch.

"My, my but we're testy this morning," said the old man. "Now, Ag, haven't I told you not to worry yourself about it. Something will work out. I'll find us a place, you'll see."

Sure! You've been saying that since Christmas, haven't you, old man? Work out—work out—everything will work out!

Now, through all of this, friend Agamemnon had not uttered more than a scratchy bleat or two, much less a word. But he might as well have spoken in complete sentences. As far as old Serendipity was concerned, he had—which is really all that mattered. After sharing a roof together for as long as these two had, they communicated quite well with one another, in their own way. At least the janitor was convinced. He was certain that he understood each sweet and surly look in those big pink-rimmed eyes, every expression of that shaggy, knobby-legged body with its low-slung belly.

The janitor made a pooh-poohing wave in the air. "You know," he said, a small grin spreading through the middle of his beard, "at times, Ag, you sound just like a shrewish old fish-wife. Sorry, but I have to say it."

The pounding whine and roar of machinery drifted down into the parlor from the street overhead. Ag drew back against the rough whitewashed wall.

Huh! Always hiding things from me, old man! Well, this is one mess you can't run away from, can you?

Old Serendipity was unaware that he could never deal with unpleasant things, brushing them from his mind whenever they came along. Peace and quiet was all he ever asked for in

his old age; an uncomplicated life in a secluded place where he could read his books, tend to his window plants, and chat with Ag now and then.

"But, Ag," the old man said, "it's not as though we're going to be thrown out into the street. I mean, haven't I worked seventeen years for the people here? The company promised to see about another job in one of their buildings—so you see? There's nothing to fret about."

He ran his eyes across a line of his botany books then began pacing slowly. "And, well . . . a change might do us good. Yes. Think of it that way, old friend. Yes. Perhaps it'll be a job in one their new buildings. Wouldn't that be something?" His voice brightened. "My, my. A bigger basement for you to roam in, no more trash cans to haul upstairs by hand. Elevators —why maybe one of those elegant marble lobbies like you see in these high rises—you know?"

Agamemnon's hoof scraped the bookcase top. If anything, his expression was now gloomier.

Speak for yourself, old man. I don't need a bigger basement; this one suits me fine, always has. Why do we have to move at all?

Why, indeed? The janitor had to ask himself. He sighed— they had been happy here. And how could he even begin to explain to Ag the whole complicated business about real estate values and Urban Renewal when he was completely unable to understand any of it himself?

Brrrrr-rackettty y-SPLAT-TATAT-TAT! An ear-splitting chorus of air hammers tore down into the street from the construction site off Tenth; work was underway again, full blast.

Rattling dishes, the sudden din shivered the old man's dentures and drove Ag in panic against the wall. The janitor had all he could do to keep from laughing at the sight.

Laugh, old man, go on. Look at your windows and laugh at the X's, why don't you?

"But, Ag," Mr. Serendipity said. "Didn't we agree just to pay no mind to all that up there? I mean, going to pieces like this every time there's noise . . ." He smiled and tapped a finger to his ear. "Now if only you'd let me put some cotton in your ears, too. These plugs help; I hardly notice any of it."

Plugs!

That was the last thing any self-respecting goat would allow to be stuffed into his ears. Agamemnon's eyes clamped shut in frustration. The more the man tried to brush off their problem, the more upset the animal became.

"Now, Ag . . ."

Don't you 'now Ag' me!

The goat bleated twice then half-slid down from the bookcase, clomping to the floor and nearly falling. Righting himself, he peered up at old Serendipity.

I just hope you know what you're doing, old man.

"It'll be all right, Ag, you'll see."

Huh! It better. Nothing I can do to get us out of this fix. I'm only a Serbian mountain goat, you know.

His head hung low, Agamemnon ambled out of the front parlor leaving the old man to himself. Mr. Serendipity stood gazing up at the maze of pipes and electrical cables which crisscrossed the ceilings as if the answer to their dilemma might be hidden up there.

Past the freshly-painted X's of the windows, a pair of young brown legs could be seen speeding a skate-scooter along the sidewalk. From this steep angle below street level, never more than the bottom halves of shopping carts or baby carriages or people could be seen passing by.

A clock chimed from somewhere in the musty recesses of the cellar beyond. Ten times, the old man counted. Chores waited to be done, he realized. By this time each day he was usually finished with hauling out the trash and sweeping the five flights of stairs in the twin-tenements. This morning however, he had no heart for work.

·EXILE·

After seventeen years . . .

His home and his job, both coming to an end all of a sudden. And in such a horrible way. Just the thought of how it would be done was enough to drive old Serendipity upstairs to the chores awaiting him. There was a dull throbbing ache at his temples.

He knew how it would be done—exactly how. Hadn't he seen it take place in stages, across the way, off Tenth Avenue where the new construction was going up? And now, months later, it was happening to 821–823 West 22nd Street, the twin-tenements. The arrival one morning of the demolition crews with those hungry machines. Burly workmen soon hack-

ing, ripping away in clouds of dust at the tired tenements, floor by floor. Until they were only shells for the bulldozers to smash and push into small mountains of broken brick and splinters.

The janitor kept busy all day; anything to keep from thinking about it. He fixed a faucet in apartment 3G, rewired the doorbell for 5E, and replaced a broken pane (for the sixtieth odd time in seventeen years) in the entrance door to 821. He hauled the garbage up to the street, rolling the cans into place next to the chalk-scribbled stoop, then mopped the hallways.

After lunch he was asked by one of the boys from 4E to help him fix his bicycle chain. With this done, the janitor delivered the empty cartons he had promised to Mrs. Jefferson on the ground floor. She was packing to move.

By the time he returned from a stroll to a shop in Greenwich Village with the new astronomy book he had bought, the light over the block was dimming. He went down the flight of rusted iron steps that led to his front door, stopping in the area-way at the bottom. Here he placed his package on the lid of an ashcan and bent over a window ledge. Like the other front basement windows, this one was packed to its warped frames with potted geraniums. Now began a daily ritual. One that the old man never failed to perform, except when it rained.

Carefully—going from leaf to leaf and bloom to bloom—Mr. Serendipity blew and brushed the city soot off his plants. The flowers soon glowed in the light which slanted from above down over blackened brick and cement. His geraniums were truly something to see. Huge, velvety-petaled blossoms, they

were startling in their shades of deep pink and scarlet.

Two women stood unnoticed on the stoop, peering down at the janitor in the stairwell below and shaking their heads in wonder. They had never been able to figure out how he did it. Neither could their neighbors. How did he manage to raise such blooms, year after year, in the face of smog, soot and traffic fumes? (While they had to watch their own house plants turn sickly, leaves yellowing, the flowers few and stunted.) They had once asked him what his secret was. "Secret?" he said with a shrug. "Oh, no ma'm, just proper care . . . And not too much watering, I guess. You know?" His reply only left the ladies more perplexed. Maybe it was that private little smile he wore which made them go off casting suspicious glances back over their shoulders.

"Queer ol' duck," whispered Mrs. Jefferson, the bigger of the two women on the stoop. "Notice how he's always so *po*lite. Notice? Always see him around, somewhere, doing some one thing or another. For years—with that funny scuffling walk of his, head tipped to one side like it does."

"Yes," her companion agreed, "always keeping to himself and smiling, like he know something nobody else does." This was the way the old man looked when lost in his thoughts which was most of the time.

"Maybe," Mrs. Jefferson said, drawing a breath, "he gets those blooms on account of he . . . *talks* . . . to the things. That's what I said. I've seen him a couple of nights, bent over those pots down there . . . *talking* to them."

The frail younger woman next to her, with arms a tint darker than the shopping bag she held, formed a silent O with her lips.

"You, *too?*" she breathed. "*Dios mio!*"

Her black lashes trembled. "Me, also. Day after my Luisa's confirmation—only I was afraid to tell nobody. Maybe they think I was loco or something." She giggled softly.

Folding her heavy arms across her bosom, Mrs. Jefferson nodded. "Been around as long as I can remember, he has, which is long. And what do any of us know about him?"

Hoisting up her groceries, Mrs. Ramirez began to cross the stoop to the other door. "New York," she sighed. "Not like in P.R. Down there on the island everybody know everybody." A sad, thin smile played on her face for a second.

The neighbors parted company, both sighing at the thought of the hectic days ahead for them. All those barrels and cartons they still had to pack before the movers came.

Mr. Serendipity finished watering his geraniums. The recorded chimes of a frozen custard truck were heard moving along the street unseen overhead. The old man bent back and peered at the sky high above the line of tenements on the opposite side of the street.

Ah . . . here they are. The toros are flying, he noted. A comforting thought at a time like this. They're *still* flying. The sight of several of these homemade kites dipping in the apricot-tinged sky, made the old man feel at peace. West 22nd Street was the same as ever. Pausing in his open doorway, he dimly recalled flying kites as a boy.

"Just some tissue and a couple of sticks," he mused. "How free it must feel, up there on a roof, holding the string . . ."

·NIGHTMARE·

On a day as fine as the next one, it was hard to believe that West 22nd was undergoing big changes.

All the commotion and racket caused by the construction at the far end of the block was over for the week. It was Saturday, and a lovelier spring morning was hard to come by. A *calinda* day, agreed the men playing dominoes in their shirtsleeves under the *bodega* awning at the corner of Ninth Avenue. They tipped their beer-cans in salute to the weather.

As always in early May, the block of tenements, rooming houses and loft buildings pulsed with activity. Another Manhattan winter was over. Life again was spilling outdoors into the streets.

Clothesline pulleys squeaking over the back-alleys, mixed with the beats of mambo, bugaloo and soul music drifting from transistors on stoops and in open windows. Big sisters hung out the wash while on the roadway below their brothers and cousins were into the third stickball game of the day. With a broomstick poised ready to swing, the stickball player is the undisputed king of the street.

Cars passing crosstown were hooted at and forced to crawl by at five miles an hour. Truck drivers could honk their horns till their palms were red, but the game stops for nothing; *or nobody, man.* Only one thought is in the head of the guy at bat—to whack that pink rubber ball for *four-sewers* in a long soaring arc heading east, over lampposts, past kids on fire escapes, and still rising, crossing above the traffic on Ninth until *smack*, it bounces off the dome of the squat church on the far side of the avenue. *Got to be, man—four-sewers—a sure homer.*

For the kids in their skin-tight T-shirts seen dotting the rooftop ledges it was one *boss-tough day* for kite-fighting. In the blue over the smokestacks and TV antennas, the toros were paired off in mortal combat. Swooping, turning, their long knotted tails went snaking after each other. Angry brilliant glints of sunlight flashed from spots along the upper sections of the kite lines where, spaced about a foot apart, slivers of double-edged razor blades were tied. At the foot of each string crouched a boy, tensely squinting upwards. Roof tar crackling under his sneakers, he would bob and weave, one hand feeding line, the other maneuvering deftly in swift short tugs— up, down, sideways. *It takes wrist action, man*, they will tell you. *The trick is to fake the other cat out, see?* To catch him

zigging when he should be zagging—then, fast, work your line across his to where the gleaming razor snips can do their work. Then, yank! If you work it right, it's bye-bye toro. And another kite, cut loose, sails high and away out over the Hudson until lost from sight above the Palisades on the Jersey side of the river.

Down on the sidewalk the mailman made his stop at the twin-tenements. Slipping a long white envelope into the box marked SERENDIPITY—SUPER, the man could not help noticing that this was the first letter he had delivered to the old guy that did not look either like a bill or an ad. It was neither.

After hunting all over for his reading glasses, old Serendipity found them perched on his head. A tingle of excitement raced up his back and into his few remaining hair roots. Agamemnon, sniffing about in the garbage pail under the sink, grew still and watched him open the letter.

"From the company people," the janitor announced in a hush.

Sure took their good time answering you.

"Oh well, Ag, one of those thing . . ." Mr. Serendipity sat down at the kitchen table and began reading aloud.

Dear Hannibal,

We have given your request for transfer to a custodial job in one of the other buildings we manage a good deal of thought. Our firm fully appreciates your long years of able service at 821-823.

The old man nodded with delight, then he read on.

And while we have a company policy limiting the age of our employees to sixty-five years, we would continue to make an exception in your case were it not for certain information brought to our attention some two years ago.

Scanning the next lines, the old man's eyes clouded and he fell silent, reading the rest to himself to spare his friend's tender feelings.

It seems that you keep a rather unusual pet. Again, due to your loyal service record, we have overlooked this until now. However, with the only job you might fill being in one of our new high rises, this presents a problem. In these buildings we only permit pets which are the standard, conventional types—those traditional kinds adaptable to modern luxury living. Thus, as you can see, you would have to give yours up if we are to further employ you. The decision is entirely up to you, of course.

Whatever you should decide, we wish you well. Please feel free to call upon us for employment references. We trust you appreciate our positon in this matter.

Enclosed find our check to cover the costs of moving and relocation. Finally, since the evacuation of 821-823 West 22nd must be completed in eight days, we suggest that you let us know your decision as soon as possible.

The letter slipped from his hand to the floor, his head beginning to ache again. How could he possibly part with *him?* Bad enough to have to uproot everthing as it is. And—why? Why must he now consider making such a choice? Those typewritten words made no sense: ". . . standard, conventional

kinds . . . adaptable to modern luxury living . . ." To his simple way of looking at things *one* was as nice as another, as long as it was the pet you wanted. Dog, parakeet, horse, frog, spider-monkey . . . what was the difference? Besides, who could it hurt? Just so long as the "type" was quiet and friendly, and nice—like Ag.

The old man watched Agamemnon paw at the letter and examined him from chin whiskers to tail. For the life of him, he failed to see a single unpleasant or hurtful thing about him. Why Ag looked every inch like a "standard, conventional" goat.

Turn you down, did they, old man?

"Huh? What?" the janitor stammered, pried from his thoughts. "Oh. Er . . ." He paused. How could he reveal the awful facts? "Why, no, well . . . not exactly."

Not exactly?

Mr. Serendipity flushed. At a loss for words, he signaled his goat to dispose of the letter which he promptly did in about six seconds.

Wish I could help out.

The old man coughed in surprise. "Help out?" he mumbled. How much did Ag know?

To find you, that is—us—a place to go.

"To go," echoed the janitor, still stalling.

Now look, old man! Will you stop hiding things from me! If they turned you down, they turned you down. No job—no place to live. Right? So wake up and find us one.

Thank heavens, thought old Serendipity with a sigh of re-lief. Then Ag doesn't know *all* of it; about the unthinkable

decision they asked him to make. Leaning forward in his chair, the janitor hugged his goat thankfully.

Still there was that throbbing in his head. The old man got to his feet, headed for his wicker rocking chair in the parlor, saying, "Think I'll read for a spell." It was all he could think to do at the moment.

Books—you and your books. The sky could be falling and you'd be buried in some book!

The answer to this new dilemma did not lie in the pages of any encyclopedia. There were twenty-one volumes in the set he owned, and he had read each one of them, taking three years to do it. He was now reading them again, just for pleasure this time around, and had reached volume FA-FR. But there was no pleasure in reading today. The words soon began to swim about on the pages. Unable to concentrate, he shut the book then gazed about him, searching for a calendar, stopping short when it struck him that he hadn't owned one in years.

Eight days left—Mr. Serendipity groaned. He turned and looked out the window, glimpsing a couch being carried by, suspended between the arms of two moving men up on the pavement. In a moment it would be loaded into a van parked at the curb, along with the other household goods of the family in 3E. And, soon, one more family would be on their way to new quarters. There'd be another empty apartment to be swept out.

Leaving the parlor and volume FA-FR behind, old Serendipity went outside. Reaching the top of the areaway staircase, he stopped, to shield his eyes against the afternoon glare.

"Heyyy Mister Seren . . . dippp!" Francie's shrill call came to him from amidst the grinding clatter of ball-bearing skate wheels. The ten-year-old waved at the janitor, her hair flying orange in the sunlight, one foot propelling her along the pavement on her skate-scooter. Mr. Serendipity returned the girl's wave, wondering how many of those fruit crates mounted on a two-by-four and skate wheels, he had helped kids put together in seventeen years.

Mr. Santiago of 3E came down the stoop, a box crammed with family utensils and religious statues in one arm, and a floor lamp in his other hand. Setting the lamp down on the sidewalk, he blew through his lips, jutting his chin up at the twin-tenements. The double five stories of dark windows painted with white Xs stared outward, the buildings looking like they had been sealed under quarantine during a deadly plague.

"*Que linda*—real pretty now, eh, Mister S.?" Mr. Santiago grinned, his thin mustache spreading. "Nine year we live here and that landlord, he don't do nothing to fix her up. Now— time to move, tear her down and boom, she gets all decorated nice!" He laughed and still wagging his head, he picked up the lamp, heading on towards the truck being loaded beyond. "*Que linda . . .*"

"Can't say these dumps are gonna be missed, eh?" Putting up his broom, the old man nodded uncertainly at Mrs. Thomas, Francie's mother, a round fleshy woman in a flower print housedress.

"Not that you haven't done your best, Mister S, to keep them from falling apart on us," she went on, taking a better grip on the small boy in her arms. "Only when a place has had it

it's had it, y'know? Glad we'll be out before the dog-days roll around, come July—you know what a steambox it gets in our place up top. The kids whining, Joe hardly fit to live with."

"We're lucky—found us a nice four-and-a-half out in Coney Island, y'know? Double-exposure—Joe's tickled. He's a fishing fool—gets anywheres close to ocean."

"You ought to like that, Timmy," the janitor said to the small boy in Mrs. Thomas' arms. "Next to the seaside and all."

"Well, things to do, things to do," Francie's mother said with a happy grimace. "Started packing a week ago, would you believe, and still at it?" She started off. "Why don't you drop up later and have a beer with us, Mister S?"

He thanked her just the same. "Some other time if it'd be all right," Mr. Serendipity added.

"Sure . . . " Mrs. Thomas went up the stoop. "Except there ain't much time left for *another* time, y'know."

That night he had planned a small celebration for his seventy-fifth birthday. As in years past, just he and Ag; mocha eclairs for dessert, some port wine with the coffee, then a good cigar. Afterwards, he would settle into his wicker rocker for that wonderful moment—unwrapping the package he had brought home the day before. A brand new astronomy book, a birthday gift to himself. He probably would stay up till well past midnight pouring over the fresh-smelling pages.

As things actually turned out, however, none of this took place. After a tasteless dinner only half-eaten, the mocha eclairs were left forgotten in the refrigerator.

The old man took the remains from his plate out to the back-

yard for the tomcat, then scratched up the earth around the rows of seedlings he had planted there in a narrow patch along the rotting fence. They stood in neat rows—tender green shoots of zinnias, petunias and marigolds, pushing up through the dark, pungent topsoil. Mr. Serendipity sprinkled the seedlings with a water can then returned inside.

His bones crackling, he did a half dozen or so knee bends, mumbled goodnight to Ag, and crawled into bed where he lay tossing for hours.

Worries and fragments of memories wrestled endlessly in his mind. When sleep finally came it was fitful, bringing with it dreams—a swirl of fearsome visions—the last of which was a full-blown nightmare. All that he remembered of it when he awoke with a start in a chill sweat, was Ag standing ten feet tall and chasing after him with an evil grin.

The old man reached out of the tangled sheets and snapped on a light. The hands of a painted china clock pointed to 2:40 A.M. Going back to sleep was out of the question. So he got dressed, splashed some water on his face, then went up into the street.

There was moonlight on West 22nd.

·NIGHTSOUNDS·

It was city air, but at this hour with a spring breeze blowing from the river, it smelled sweet. The old man slowly filled his lungs.

To either side of him the block lay empty, long and cool-dark with pools of lamplight; some newspaper pages skittering along the far curb. A sprinkle of car headlights moved along the raised expressway that bordered the Hudson, three blocks west, crosstown. Crossing the street, diagonally towards Tenth, he reached the construction site which ran nearly a third of the way up the block from the corner, and downtown, through to West 21st Street.

A tall fence made up of plywood panels and old doors hid

most of the first floor of the towering steel framework. Beyond it could be seen eight more floors of bare steelwork; a complex of orange-painted I-beams, massive girders laid with heavy planking at each landing. All nine stories of the construction were criss-crossed with scaffolding and catwalks, and festooned everywhere with all sorts of pipe, rods and cables. Flanking the site were a pair of derricks rising at an angle, their soaring crane-necks of latticed steel hung with pulleys making them look like gigantic praying-mantises.

Old Serendipity's eyes strayed up the construction, its painted steel now wine-red in the moonlight. He saw an un-finished staircase which ran zig-zag through the steelwork only to end in nowhere. While putting a match to his pipe he heard a set of clomping footsteps coming from across the way.

He turned and grinned sadly. "Couldn't sleep either, eh? Hm. Wonder what it was you dreamed."

Ag came to a stop under a lamppost.

We don't dream.

"Is that so?" the janitor said with some surprise. "Seems to me, seems I read somewhere that animals do—dream, that is."

I don't know anything about animals, only goats.

They both noticed the sound at about the same time. A curious sort of musical tootling was coming from somewhere above. The old man craned his head back and peered about. Following the tootling he traced it up into the steelwork and began to search its jumble of shadowy forms. It sounded like . . . a harmonica? Yes, that's what it was all right, he realized. Abruptly, the music stopped, replaced by a raspy chuckle which hit a shrill peak and broke off.

This was followed by: "One *reeel* pretty night, wouldn't y'all say? Yeah . . ." The voice from on high was gravelly, a dusky drawl, sly, mocking and tinged with laughter.

Agamemnon bleated, backing away. Old Serendipity crossed the road to him, then cupping his hand to his mouth, called, "Please don't stop playing on my account, sir."

He heard a snort in return. "I don't start on nobody's account," came the voice, "and I don't stop on nobody's account, man. Only on C. H. Mackelgum's account."

The janitor exchanged an uncertain glance with Ag. He scanned the landings of the steelwork seeking the voice's owner. The harmonica began to play again: a string of breathy chugging chords pierced with little wails from time to time. The melody was like that of a lonesome train, now coming down the line, now turning a bend.

The old man spied a bright sting of light, the chrome of the harmonica flashing, then movement . . . along a catwalk up on the fifth floor. The train-blues slowed and stopped. And a short silhouetted figure was seen waving downward.

"There—see me now, friend?"

Mr. Serendipity returned the wave. "Yes, yes, now I do. Evening, sir—that was certainly fine playing."

"Yeah . . ." the figure muttered softly, sitting down on the edge of the catwalk and dangling its feet in space. Some moments of silence passed before the stranger extended his arm.

"Look like, pretty soon now," he called, pointing down the street towards 822-824, "they be busting up your place, too."

The old man swallowed and shot his palms outward with a shrug.

"All these new glass and stone boxes they putting up," the figure on high said, "look like a lot of skyhigh filing cabinets to me, with their drawers stuck out."

He must mean the terraces, thought Mr. Serendipity. His head bobbed in agreement. "Going up all over these days—hardly for poor folks like us."

"Not *me*, man," sang the stranger. "Uh *uh!* I'm broke—good and broke—but never poor, man, never. Say, that down there with you sure look like a fine hound dog."

Still caught up trying to figure out the difference between being "broke" and "poor", the janitor was taken aback. "Oh," he finally replied. "Guess you mean Ag here. He's hardly a dog, sir."

Chuckles rolled down from the construction, then: "All right, all right. Hope nobody's feelings are hurt."

Mr. Serendipity saw Ag's eyes glisten hotly.

My feelings, old man!

"Now, now, Ag." The janitor patted his head.

"What'd y'all say?"

"Nothing," the janitor mumbled, then called, "A goat—he's a goat."

"A . . ." There was a stunned silence above. "Whoo-weee! You don't say. Know'd a fella up on a Hundred Twenty-Third who had him a pet skunk—but never no city person with no goat." The stranger laughed. "I'm a country man myself; you can have the city."

A car drove by, a quick gleam under the lamplight, its tires thunking over manhole covers. When quiet returned the harmonica tooted again. This time it had a slower, soulful

sound, humming a down-home blues, one that had no beginning or end. Born in the backwaters of the South somewhere long past, it now wove its way through the clotheslines of West 22nd.

"All right, all right," the stranger said when he finished. "I didn't exactly catch your name . . ."

"Oh," the old man called. "Hannibal—Hannibal Serendipity, sir."

"You don't say." The silhouetted figure stood up. "C. H. Mackelgum, here," it announced. "Baptized Clinton Hezekiah. C.H. to most. Middle name—got you a middle?"

Old Serendipity grinned at Ag.

Dare you to tell him, old man.

The janitor again cupped a hand to his mouth. "Servatius, that's with an S. It's Swiss."

After a silent moment gleeful laughter broke out on the fifth floor of the steelwork, echoing along the slumbering block.

"No offense, man," the stranger explained when he quieted: "But it's taken me a whole lotta lifetime to meet up with a man what got himself given a fool-funnier name than mine!"

When Hannibal Servatius Serendipity went back to bed later, he was very ready for sleep.

Thin silver light was starting to seep into the cellar from behind the window shades as he turned his face into the cool pillow. He did not know why it was, but he felt an odd sort of kinship to the short dark figure up in the steelwork.

The following morning, for the first time in seventeen years,

he did not wake at his usual dawn hour. The neighborhood kids had already been in school for two hours when Agamemnon licked his ear and finally woke him.

.GOODBYES.

For Francie, for Leroy, Cruz, Junie and all the other kids in the twin-tenements who had grown up on West 22nd, moving meant being taken away. To the unknown. It meant being separated from old pals and hangouts: the rooftops and alleys and haunts along the riverfront that they knew so well they could move through them blindfolded. Awaiting were alien, uncharted turfs. Places inhabited by strangers: new teachers, classmates, cops, stickball hustlers, the block bully—and who knew *what all?*

"*There?*" Junie said uneasily, in answer to his younger brother's query as they loaded suitcases into their uncle's car. "S'got to be a whole other scene, man, where we're goin' ."

32

So, racing against time, the ring-a-leavio and skelly players would try to squeeze in one more game before the call came for them to leave. *Just one more, Ma, just one!* Coiling into tighter crouches over their bottle-cap shooters, the skelly players took hasty aim for the next numbered box on the chalk field, hoping to get one more killer—the kind of shot that made your girlfriend's eyes bug out. And the stickball players pleaded: "Aw, Maaa, after my licks, Ma. I'm up next!"

For a blinky, naive old man who'd lived closed off from the world for so long, moving was a bewildering and rather painful task. It meant finding both a new job and a place to live.

Mr. Serendipity went about it in the only way he knew. He began the days checking the classified newspaper ads, then walked the streets inquiring at local real estate management offices. He did try, in his timid way. Still, with only three days left before demolition, he had found nothing. Nothing available to someone like him, that is.

821-823 West 22nd was now the scene of feverish disorder upstairs. Most families had already moved out and the few remaining were in some last-minute stage or another of doing so. In his basement parlor, old Serendipity sat with one ear cocked to the noises overhead and the other to the telephone receiver in his hand.

"Say—exactly how old are you?"

The voice at the other end of the phone was thick and demanding. It was nearing the end of the business day; time enough for only one or two more calls. As always, each time he dialed another real estate office, his hope would flicker.

"Well . . ." the janitor said, hesitating. That question—the same one again, he thought.

"I said, how—"

"Yes sir," Mr. Serendipity rushed to say. "Why, er, three-score-and-fifteen, and never felt fitter, sir." He ended with a nervous little chuckle.

"*What?*"

"Why, seventy-five last week and not a sick day in the last twenty. No, sir."

"Yeah . . . ?"

A hanging stillness came to the receiver at his ear. If only there was something he could say, something that would impress the man that *he* was *just* the man for the job.

Finally, he heard: "Well . . . we run a building over on the Upper West Side . . . we might give you a try at. Maybe."

Mr. Serendipity's heart leaped. "Oh," he sang out. "You'd have no regrets, sir, not a one. And and no charge for Ag, either. You can ask anyone how he loves children, and there's no better way to keep your basement and alleys clean. He's a real scavenger, he is."

"What was that?"

"Ag—my goat," Mr. Serendipity said, beaming.

"*Boat?*"

"No, sir," the old man hastened to explain. "Goat, sir; descendant of a truly noble breed of Serbian mountain—"

CLICK.

He was left with a dead phone. "Hello? Hel . . . lo?" The janitor's voice shriveled. Staring numbly at the receiver, he let it drop into the cradle. Ag looked across at him from the

divan, where, lying folded, he looked like a gray hairy sack with hooves and ears.

Did it again, didn't you, old man?

"Did?" the old man echoed, befuddled.

I give up. I don't be-lieve you!

Mr. Serendipity looked stunned. "Believe me? But . . . but every word I told the man was the truth."

I give up, old man. Ag bleated in weary frustration.

"Now, see here," the janitor said, reddening. "If all you can do is lie there and—and belittle my efforts. I'm doing the best I can." He slumped down in his chair.

Ag, slipping to the floor, crawled under the divan where he remained, no doubt wondering about what it was like in the mountains of Serbia those days.

The minutes ticked by, the old man pondering the choices left to him, suddenly aware that they had boiled down to only one now. As his thoughts ran in endless circles his sighs grew longer. After awhile, certain thoughts—thoughts which up to then had been unthinkable—began stealing into his head: Poor Ag, poor fellow. Who got him into this mess, anyhow? All these years, keeping him cooped up in a city basement. Why he belongs on a . . . on a farm someplace, that's where. Yes . . . he deserves shade trees and a field of clover. Hmmm . . . Perhaps I could find some nice farmer who would—or, maybe—a zoo? That Children's Zoo in Central Park? They have barn-yard animals, likely other goats, too. Laughing children to feed him every day. Yes. Ag would love that!

Glancing down at the floor, Mr. Serendipity discovered a pair of glistening eyes peering up into his from under the

edge of the divan. The eyes, boring right into him, made the old man wince and turn away with guilt and shame.

The curbside before the twin-tenements was lined with moving vans, pickup trucks and haul-it-yourself trailers hitched to cars. One no sooner left when another pulled up into its place. The lucky tenants who could afford to, hired movers, the others did the job themselves. A scraggly parade of people perspiring under their loads went squeezing past one another on stairways and up and down the adjoining stoops. While all the time small children were underfoot on the pavement, forever chalk-drawing names and faces as if nothing special were going on.

On the afternoon of the next to the last day, old Serendipity stood leaning against the railing above the areaway. Francie, a few paces away, a plastic doll-case clasped in her arms, watched him from the corner of her eyes. After twice starting to say something, only to stop, she said, "Going pretty soon now, Mister Serendip."

The old man watched her work up a bubble with the gum in her mouth. "Mm," he nodded. "Yes, pretty soon."

Francie's bubble popped. Drawing the gum back in, she came over to him.

"Um . . ." She paused and squinted. "Um, like late at night, I mean, did you ever hear funny music? I mean, playing? Late?" the girl added. "From way up there, somewhere?" She pointed upwards down the street towards the steel construction. "Like a harm . . . onica or something?"

The janitor's eyebrows shot up in surprise. "From way up . . ."

"Uh huh."

"Now—whatever would you be doing up at that hour, Francie?"

Francie's eyes glittered. "So then you did, too? You heard it! I thought first it was a radio, or I was dreaming, y'know? It sounded so cool."

Mr. Serendipity saw her father and oldest brother beyond, hitching up the tailgate of the truck they'd finished loading. "No," he said with a tug at his suspenders. "It was a real harmonica you heard. Seems there's some nice fellow who likes to sit up there at night when its quiet, and play."

The truck horn sounded a summons to the girl. About to speak again, she broke off and started away to the curb. Pausing for a moment, she darted back a shy smile of farewell, then ran off, calling, "Hope Aga . . . memnon has a yard or something . . . where you're moving!"

After the truck had pulled away, Francie's pale arm waving back at him from the cab window, the janitor drew a list of tenants out of his back pocket. He ran the tip of a pencil down the column of long-familiar family names, stopping at THOMAS, 5H. Slowly, he drew a dark wavy line through the letters.

His eyes scanned the list. That's it, he sighed to himself. All of the twenty-four family names were now crossed out. And, like the captain of an abandoned ship, Hannibal Serendipity was the last one left on board.

·SCHEMERS·

"How y'all making it, Hann . . . ibul?"

Again that voice, sounding higher this time but just as sly and gravelly. He was happy to hear it; he had been unable to sleep at all that night. Dropping his head back, old Serendipity peered up into the fine mist rolling from the river.

He shrugged. "Oh, pretty well, I guess, all things considered. You sound in fine fettle, though."

A chord of the harmonica like a quick chuckle came in reply. Shielding his eyes from the lamplight, the janitor saw the figure step out on a cross-tie up on the sixth floor.

"Yeah . . . Anybody readier has got to go by me. How's that billy goat of yours?" the voice called.

Mr. Serendipity waved to indicate Ag was well. After some small talk the stranger on high said, "Getting plain foolish our talking this way, ain't it? Keep it up and we both gonna lose our voices—and your head's in danger of dropping off, twisting it back like you doing. Now if you was up here . . ."

The old man jerked backwards. "Up there?"

"Shucks! Nothing to get discommoded about. Anything brings us a little closer to heaven can't be bad." A flashlight was seen to go on, its beam dancing over a corner post.

"Listen," the voice instructed, "stay put, friend, I'm going round to the other side. Be down for y'all in a minute—y'hear?" The figure disappeared into the darkness.

Old Serendipity stood fidgeting on the wooden walk along the foot of the fence, now hearing the dull whine of a motor and cables running over pulleys. The noise soon stopped, and in moments footsteps came, approaching from beyond the fence. There was the squeak of hinges and suddenly the flashlight beam poked through an open door some ten yards down the boardwalk.

"Don't worry now," he heard, the beam glancing into his eyes. "I'm the one in charge here—the onlyiest one at this hour, man—night watchie, see? Yeah, ole Mackelgum the watchie," the stranger announced self-mockingly. "Evening, Hann . . . ibul."

Mr. Serendipity glimpsed a gold tooth among the gaps in the smile that came at him as he arrived. Before he knew it, the stranger's hand shot out and he felt his hand clasped by a stubby, callused palm with a grip like spring-steel. Why, thought the janitor, he must be almost as old as me. It was dif-

ficult to tell how old, but plainly C. H. Mackelgum had traveled a long, hard road in his time.

A short, rawboned, bantam of a man, the watchman's narrow shoulders were sloped from labor and his legs slightly bowed. The dark skin of his neck was leathery, and the bald dome of his head, fringed with white hair, shone in the lamplight. But it was the watchman's eyes that one noticed first. Set deeply in wrinkled pouches, they were amber-colored and their gaze was keenly alive and challenging.

"Enter, enter, my man." Mr. Mackelgum directed with a sweep of the flashlight.

Mr. Serendipity found himself drawn after the stranger, trailing him uneasily across the work site past stacks of equipment and supplies.

"Yeah," said the watchman while moving. "You the super of those two across the road waiting to get busted up—right? Yeah, I know, I know. Well, that's how it goes."

The flashlight stopped, revealing a caged-in work lift, the sort used to run men and supplies up the steelwork during the day. Mr. Serendipity was waved inside. He saw the man shut the wire-mesh door, then press a lever. The lift began to rise. "Takes a mite under two minutes to the top—more with both of us, I expect," the watchman said.

To the top? Old Serendipity blinked nervously, watching the floors slowly drop by them, the canvas-covered supplies lying about each stage looking like a sleeping army.

"Er . . . pleasant job you have, sir," the janitor finally said. "Quiet and all."

"Outdoors at least," said the watchman, snorting. "Cooped-

up work ain't for me. Only temporary though." He made a sniff of satisfaction. "Gave the Man my quitting notice last week."

The foggy moon drew closer. Noticing some faint clicks coming from the janitor's beard, Mr. Mackelgum grinned.

"Be getting me a set of them store teeth one of these days, I guess," he said, to his passenger's surprise. "These last six of mine can't do much." His chuckle was lost in the clunk made by the work lift as it bounced to a stop. The cage door opened. Pointing the way with the light beam Mr. Mackelgum stepped out, calling, "Straight on, straight on . . . only mind your steps."

There was nothing above but the pale vaporous night; nine stories and some hundred and fifty feet below were the streets. Mr. Serendipity crossed the platform of heavy planking, moving gingerly, past stacked supplies and timber, coils of heavy cable, rolls of mesh and a host of shapes he could not make out in the darkness. Here and there glowed a few watch-lanterns. "Up this away," he heard. Moving towards the voice, he reached the stairway that ended in nowhere and saw the watchman seating himself on the uppermost landing.

"Sometimes," mused the dark man, "when it's still like now, I like to think I'm top of one our hills down home. Sometimes, I almost think so—but not for long. City, man, city."

He motioned for Mr. Serendipity to take a seat, but he chose to stand a step below. The speckle of lights that stretched out far below seemed to swim like pinwheels in the mist. Mr. Mackelgum saw the janitor wag his head and sigh.

"All X'd up and waiting," the watchman said. "Well, life's

full of changes. Keeps you on your toes at our age—if you're *ready*. I'm moving on myself, like I said, with no regrets, man, not a one."

"Gonna miss it, eh?" he added.

Mr. Serendipity nodded dismally.

"Got you a tight little spot down there?"

Again the janitor nodded. Withdrawing his pipe, he told how his apartment was the coolest one in summer and the warmest of all in winter, in the basement like it was. "Seventeen years," he murmured, "with a place for everything."

"And everything in it's place," Mr. Mackelgum completed. "Know what you saying."

"Say," the watchman remarked abruptly, lowering the harmonica from his lips, "you eighty yet, friend?" His eyes glittered cannily.

"Huh?" the janitor mumbled. "Oh. Why, no—seventy-five."

"Hm, thought you eighty at least. Guess, man, that's because you look so down, so down. Hey," the watchman jutted his face forward, "how old you figger C.H. here is. Eh? Go on, say it."

Mr. Serendipity creased and uncreased his forehead. "Well," he stammered, "about like me, I suppose, maybe a year or two . . . younger?"

"Eighty-two," announced the watchman. "Y'all heard me—eighty and *two*, that's right. And ready. Know what I'm saying?"

The janitor shook his head, puzzled.

"For whatever comes down the road," Mr. Mackelgum rumbled. "Man, I been around too long, been through too

much to let things get the jump on me. Tell me, Hann . . . ibul, you got any bad habits—whiskey, anything like that messing you up?"

"A little rheumatiz now and then in the back."

"*That* all? Damn! Educated fella your age without no bad habits messing him up, and with a paid-up set of store teeth, shouldn't have no trouble then. Taking things as they come along."

The other man's chuckle made him uneasy. The janitor looked upwards and changing the subject, noted that no stars were to be seen. "You could see Orion clearly the other night." He sat down heavily on the stair landing.

"You don't say," Mr. Mackelgum said. "You know about stars, man?"

The janitor shook his head. "Only from books."

They spoke of the stars, their talk then turning to astrology, ancient beliefs, the mysteries of the pyramids. Mention of the thousands of slaves used to build them, caused the watchman to remark that his father as a boy had been sold to a Louisiana plantation owner and that his mother, too, had been a slave. Moving north after the Civil War, the Mackelgums became share-croppers for a tobacco landlord in Virginia. It wasn't until he had married at sixteen, the watchman said, that he had moved again, up to Maryland, where he now had "a raggedy li'l dirt farm. I get some good things out of her though— mostly corn, yams and rhubarb." The farm was being run by his daughter and her husband while he was in New York, visiting his oldest daughter. "Then her man took sick—bad. So I stayed around to look after the kids. I'm a fair hand with a

skillet, leastways her little ones didn't complain."

The janitor listened to the watchman tell how he had taken the night job to help pay off the doctor bills after his son-in-law came home from the hospital. "Yeah," he ended, "can't wait to get back to country air." Placing the harmonica to his mouth, he began to play softly.

"Eviction," Mr. Serendipity sighed, the word lingering in the air. Then he told of the sorry trouble he was in. "In two days," he groaned, standing up. "Out in the street, Ag and me . . . and everything."

Mr. Mackelgum glanced down at the time-keeper's clock that was linked to his belt. "Almost three," he said. "Hear what I said? Have to make my rounds soon."

Mr. Serendipity stood peering sadly out over the dark streets below. "There must be some place."

The watchman got to his feet, saying, "See any electrical signs out there advertising *where?*" He fixed the speechless janitor with a baleful eye. "Of course, you don't. Man, you just wasting your time. Yeah, feeling sorry for yourself instead of . . ."

"Sorry for . . ."

"Instead of listening to what I was saying. You been too busy hearing yourself moan and groan, and moan some more. And that don't accomplish nothin'."

"But, I was, . . . listening."

The watchman swatted the air. "Y'all hear me tell I give in my notice to the Man?"

Mr. Serendipity shrugged, hands pushing deeper into his pockets.

"That I was quitting?" Mr. Mackelgum declared.

"Quitting?"

"My job, man!"

"Job . . ."

"Whoo-wee!" exploded the watchman, wagging his head in amused disbelief. "Your ears plugged up or something?"

A foolish grin came over old Serendipity's face. He nodded, explaining what he meant.

Chortles rolled from the dark man. He slapped his thigh. "You something else, Hanni . . . bul! Tell me, you think you good for anything other than janitoring?" he said, giving the janitor a teasing poke. "I mean, with all that fine book-learning of yours."

From somewhere across Manhattan a tower clock struck three. "Now," Mr. Mackelgum said with a gleam. He leaned over the stair rail and waved down at the construction site, saying, "Between us, we got what? About a hundred-fifty-some odd years of living—that right? Okay, then, can't let that much wisdom go to waste, can we?"

Old Serendipity nodded uncertainly, a pounding starting in his chest. When he sat down again, questions came tumbling from him.

"All right, all right," Mr. Mackelgum said, simmering him down. "Let's see what we can work out here."

The pair of old men stayed on top of the stairway that ended in nowhere, speaking together until the tower clock across town struck four.

.O.K. POP.

"See, Ag!" old Serendipity crowed, rousing his friend the next morning to tell him the news. "It's going to work out for us after all. Clinton Hezekiah Mackelgum, that fellow up in the steelwork promised to take care of everything himself, personally."

Sure. See to everything. How—when he can't even see the difference between me and a dog?

The janitor had no time to argue; there were things to be done; he was to meet the man at the main gate at four. Humming a strain from *The Mikado*, he wrestled a dusty steamer trunk out of a closet and removed his only suit from it. After shaving carefully, he trimmed his beard and put on his only

white shirt, pleased to find he still remembered how to prop-
erly knot a tie.

The suit smelled of camphor and felt tight in several places;
but there was bounce to his step as he walked to the main gate
of the construction site, over on West 21st.

The afternoon sun was hot when he arrived. Pacing the rut-
ted ground inside the gate for a half-hour, he anxiously brushed
dust from his sleeves and ran a finger inside his starched shirt-
collar. The steelwork was clamoring with activity at every
level; workmen, their hardhats spots of silver and yellow, ham-
mering home rivets, driving nails, and hauling supplies everywhere.

At last Mr. Serendipity saw the red door of a long shed
marked *Engineering Office*, open. Stepping out onto the
wooden porch, C. H. Mackelgum waved, then loped down the
steps, coming quickly to his side.

"Set, man," he said in a triumphant hush and patted the
janitor's arm. "Starting tomorrow, how's that? Like I said
the rest's up to y'all, right?" His forehead glowed like burnished
copper in the sun.

"How—how," stammered the grateful janitor, not quite
certain what it was, that was up to him, "can I ever thank you,
C.H.?"

Mr. Mackelgum swiped at the air, turning to see the construction foreman step out onto the shed porch beyond.

"Er . . ." Mr. Serendipity murmured absently. "Did you
happen to mention Ag?"

The watchman's head spun round. "You daft?" He stepped
away to meet the foreman coming towards them, calling,

"Here's your man, you couldn't find you better! Uh uh! Trim and fit, no bad habits, and ready. Hanni . . . bul's his name, you can forget the rest—worse'n mine."

The foreman, a tall sun-reddened man in knee boots and a white hardhat, tapped a roll of blueprints at his chin eyeing the janitor.

"Okay, pop," he rumbled, "looks like you're *it*. Show him around, C.H." The foreman then turned toward the watchman. "Just so long as he's available around the clock," he said to Mr. Mackelgum. "Gonna be a twenty-four hour job for the next coupla weeks, maybe."

"Your lucky day, Mister Hatfield!" the watchman piped. "Free as a bird, he is. Nobody waiting up nights for him."

Old Serendipity smiled shyly. "Except Aga—" He gulped on the word as, glancing down, he saw it was Mr. Mackelgum's foot that had stamped on his toe. The watchman had him by the arm, fingers digging into his elbow, and was nudging him forward.

"Don't worry none, Mister Hatfield!" Mr. Mackelgum forced a smile. "I'll have your man checked out on things before the whistle."

The foreman squinted dubiously after them for a moment. "Put those clothes away for Sundays, pop," he called. "Just bring a sharp pair of eyes and ears along with you."

When they were safely out of sight, Mr. Mackelgum wheeled on his companion. "You living in a dream?" he snapped. "Man! almost like you *want* to mess things up. Here we got things set right—a strike starting up to boot—and you goes shooting off your mouth!"

Old Serendipity looked at his shoes, mumbling that he was sorry if he said anything wrong.

"Sorry! Keep that up and you gone sorry yourself into the poor peoples' house, and that animal of yours into some glue factory!" Mr. Mackelgum began jabbing his finger about them in the air. "See them trucks? Real. Nine floors of steel rising. Real. Men, machines, all real. This is a rough world you in!" Mr. Serendipity's head moved with every point made as if he were recoiling under blows.

"Got to get yourself together, Hanni . . . bul, get that cellar dust out of your eyes!" When the watchman had finished berating the janitor, he stood fuming.

After a long moment, Mr. Serendipity grinned sheepishly. "Agamemnon," he said. "He's real, too."

The watchman's jaw dropped and he wagged his head in stupified admiration. They strolled on, Mr. Mackelgum pointing out the various toolbins and supply hampers which had to be locked at the end of each day, then checked at night.

"Yeah," he said, "I guess we become worrisome ol' coots to people." He laughed, his eyes wrinkling craftily. "My daughter's always after me—scolding for this or that—like I was a kid. Yeah . . . what we is, we is."

When they had completed the tour of the site, the pair paused to watch a crane-load of steel swaying slowly up to the uppermost floor; eight tons of orange I-beams against the cool blue sky.

"That's about the last load they gonna get hoisted for a time," the watchman noted. "Closing whistle blows and everybody—I mean riveters, iron mongers, carpenters, the lot—

walks off the job. And ain't nobody knows when they coming back again. Strike, man, strike."

Mr. Serendipity sipped a breath, looking about at the vast site. "All of this . . . shut down?"

"Thought you'd like to hear. Wasn't sure about it—only rumors it'd happen, till today. Shut down tight, man. Tighter than a bigot-deputy's mind."

"I see." The janitor nibbled the edge of his moustache.

Motioning him to follow, the watchman limped on, saying, "The Lord frequently helps those which *have* to help their-selves."

He then showed the newly-hired watchman how to bolt and secure the main gate facing West 21st. Along the curb directly outside it stood a large trailer, another construction office. It would be towed away for the strike's duration, Mr. Mackelgum pointed out.

"Not this one though," he said, indicating the long wooden shed with the red door which stood inside the fence. "Tin roof, john, even a two-burner cooker; comfy office the Man has his-self."

They exchanged a quick glance.

"So, you be keeping a par-tic-ular eye on it." Mr. Mackel-gum nodded somberly. "Y'hear? Don't be letting any tramps in now."

Mr. Serendipity studied his unsmiling face. "No tramps," he repeated.

"No tramps."

The new watchman saw the outgoing one's face remain neutral, save for the eyes where tiny lights flickered. Then,

slowly, one old man triggering the other, they began laughing together like a couple of boys.

A few hours later, sounds never before heard coming up from the basement under the twin-tenements came drifting into the street above—boisterous laughing mixed with the strains of a harmonica.

Old Serendipity had a guest to dinner. There were more than enough reasons for a celebration this time, and the host outdid himself, cooking a fine roast and corn dumplings. C. H. Mackelgum, a most appreciative guest, had second helpings of both. Mocha eclairs were served for dessert, then some mellow port with the coffee and twenty-five cent cigars.

As the parlor room filled with cigar smoke, the guest treated his two hosts to a harmonica concert. Agamemnon, his eyes lidded and still, lay listening on the floor. There was a moment when Mr. Serendipity thought of young Francie, wondering whether the girl with orange hair would ever again hear such tender music in her dreams.

.SPIES.

Forty-by-eight feet, as long and narrow as a freight car, the construction shed could hardly be called a home. However, when things go wrong, then right at last—it can readily become one. Late the next night, during the departing watchman's last tour of duty, moving got underway. Using a pair of handtrucks that once hauled trashcans, the two old men made a number of trips back and forth across the street, transferring the janitor's belongings. Then, after transplanting his backyard seedlings into several empty crates, these and his geraniums were rolled to the shed by way of the back door in the construction fence.

"Man . . !" said Mr. Mackelgum when he first spotted Mr.

Serendipity's marvelous blossoms. "Your head may be up in the clouds, but look like you do pretty well in the earth!"

Mr. Serendipity only sniffed. "Something I seem to have a feel for."

At daybreak, they were finished. The geranium pots now stood lining the porch outside the red door. Resting from their labors, the pair sat tilted back in chairs, sipping tea brewed on the shed burner. A low drone came from the city just beginning to stir beyond the fence.

"All right, all right," Mr. Mackelgum said. He drained his cup, and tipping forward in his chair, got up. "I better be getting some shut-eye before that bus of mine leaves."

The new watchman sputtered, trying to put his thanks into words.

Mr. Mackelgum cut him off. "Now and again, if you have a mind to, just drop me a postal card." Stretching, he looked at Agamemnon who came wandering forward from behind a parked bulldozer. "Can't promise you an answer that'll read perfect—my spelling ain't none the best—but I'll get an answer to you." He heard a bleat come from the goat. "Making hungry sounds, eh?"

Mr. Serendipity squinted, studying Ag's expression. "No," he said flatly. "Telling you to take good care of yourself, Mister Mackelgum. Also that he'll see to it that I do a proper job here."

The dark man smiled. "Said all that, did he?"

Mr. Serendipity nodded seriously.

"I do b'lieve," Mr. Mackelgum said as they walked to the main gate, "that goat of yours was appointed to keep an eye on you; could be by ol' Noah himself."

They paused out on the wooden sidewalk and shook hands. For the last time, old Serendipity thought, feeling the iron grip of that rough bony hand.

The former watchman started down the street. "Now you take care of things, pop . . ." he called, his chuckle trailing off. Soon his figure was lost among the gather of early subway-riders at the far end of the block.

Too keyed up by the sudden newness of it all, old Serendipity did not go to bed. Instead, he went to work putting his belongings away and getting the shed into some sort of order.

At noon, a group of five striking workmen arrived outside the main gate. With cardboard picket signs strung over their shoulders, they meandered up and back along the boardwalk, joking among themselves while listening to the ballgame over a transistor radio. At five, they left for the day.

And at six, pleased and weary, Mr. Serendipity set one of his alarm clocks to wake him for his first nightwatch.

Cement, lime, tar and kerosene—a host of new aromas greeted his nostrils as he lay in bed. But the reassuring sounds of his clock and Agamemnon's rhythmic snoring lulled him into a deep sleep.

By the close of the first week the seedlings had sprouted a second rank of leaves. The early May weather was balmy and gave the old man zest for work.

With the construction work halted, passers-by stopped no longer to look through holes in the fences. When it had been going on full blast, people were always taking time out to stop

and watch. With cascades of blinding sparks no longer shower-
ing down from welders' torches, and the hammers silent, the
daily stream of gawkers and idlers ended. People passed by
again, as usual, eyes vaguely focused on the ground, rushing on
to somewhere—New Yorkers on the go. Looking, yet rarely
seeing what was about them on their way as they walked on by,
to wherever.

Using materials salvaged from the twin-tenements, the new
watchman cleverly cut down some curtains he had found left
behind in 5F and placed them on the row of small windows
inside the shed. He tacked a patchwork of three different lino-
leums over the rough floor. One of his choice finds was a hammock in 3A. He promptly strung it from a post of the shed
to the bulldozer. Here, swaying gently, he would lie and
read, or, by night, just loll and think of the past, memories
wafting like tatters of pale gauze within him.

When the twin-tenements were shells ready to fall under the
assaults of the bulldozers across the way, the old man found he
had far milder pangs of regret than he had expected.

He looked forward to the nightwatches which he began at
eleven and ended at four A.M. During these hours the lot took
on a mysterious look, and on moonlit nights, an enchanted
look. From a seat up in the steelwork, it could have been a
prehistoric landscape he was looking down on, the remains
of some ancient civilization, or the landscape of some planet as
yet unknown.

During the daytime the handful of pickets who spent the
hours strolling before the fence would occasionally nod at the
old man then return to listen to the ball game. They couldn't

care less about anything behind the fence. With his books now stored neatly away and his house in neat order, the days began to melt one into the next with an uneventful sameness. Mr. Serendipity began to feel restless midway in the second week.

After breakfast one morning, he bent and picked up a long-handled mason's trowel from the littered ground. With no special thought in mind, just something to do, he began to clear the earth in front of the shed. Ag was off greeting the tomcat who, after days of futile sniffing for them on the far side of 21st Street, finally found the good sense to cross the street and search the lot.

The soil around the construction site was packed and crusted. Better than four acres of it, the old man figured. "So much of it, just lying around," he said aloud. "Sort of a shame."

He looked at his crates of seedlings; they were about due for transplanting. "What would it hurt?" he said to himself. The place would only be covered by rank weeds in a few weeks.

Getting the tools was easy; he selected what he needed from a locker alongside one of the derricks, and quickly found a roll of wire and some fine mesh. Deciding on a plot on the sunny side of the shed, Mr. Serendipity staked out a section ten yards long by five across. He then turned the soil by spade several times, ridding it of large stones and metal shards. Next, he sifted the earth through a framed sheet of mesh until even the small stones and bits of glass were strained out. This took the better part of two days. On the evening of the last one, he took

a wheelbarrow and rolled it crosstown, west to the docks along the Hudson.

River silt—this rich, damp, black stuff had made such fine potting soil for his geraniums. As he had thought when he had first come across it years before, it *had* to be good for planting; there was so much in it. The smell was enough to tell him this. Finely powdered, the silt lay everywhere around the piers by the water. Made up of every imaginable kind of city waste and flotsam, the stuff was a decayed accumulation of industrial sludge, gull-droppings, fruit peels, leaves, coffee grounds, rat teeth, coal dust—one would never know what all. Safe to say, river silt was composed of a bit of everything in New York, and some of all that the four winds blew in from land and sea over the ages.

The old man carted back several loads of it. He then spread a deep cover of the pungent blackness to a depth of four inches over his garden plot. Into this he transplanted his marigold, zinnia and petunia seedlings.

From time to time during the month the desk phone rang. It was always Mr. Hatfield, the construction foreman, his voice brusque and business-like:

"Hatfield here—how goes it, pop?"

What could he reply? There was never anything to report. "Oh, why just fine, sir."

"Any problems?"

Problems? "No . . ." the old man would say, thinking hard. "None at all, Mister Hatfield. All's quiet."

"Okay, keep a sharp eye on the store, pop. We'll be rolling

soon." Old Serendipity would hang up, uneasy at the last words.

Perhaps he was becoming hard of hearing, but as he worked in his garden he did not seem to catch the shrill sounds that began coming from behind the fence. More than likely though, the old man was ignoring them. Delighted with the way the seedlings were taking hold, he prepared another section of ground for vegetables. "The land's going to waste, wouldn't you say, Ag?"

Agamemnon heard the giggles and sniggers coming from behind the fence, and said nothing.

"Some cukes, or beans and tomatoes would do fine; maybe even squash," the old man said, caught up in his thoughts.

Suit yourself, I prefer alfalfa myself.

Mr. Serendipity said that he didn't think that would grow here, and was about to suggest clover when the first beer can came. Lofting up over the fence, it flashed, spinning in the sunlight, then crashed onto the metal shed roof.

Ag bolted for cover. Rolling to the ground, the beer can came to a stop at the old man's feet.

"Weirdo!"

Along with this shriek, a fusillade of empty beer cans came raining onto the roof and all round the shocked watchman. He stumbled about, shielding his head with his bent arms. A soda bottle spun and shattered against the bulldozer.

"Weird—weird—WEIRDO!" Shrill laughter filled the spring air.

His tormentors stood planted out on the boardwalk in a cluster, slouched and swaying lightly, and waiting.

The oldest, about thirteen, had ballpoint tattoos on both forearms and an unblinking smile. Mugging and darting eye signals at one another, the youths held their snickers at-ready. The two girls among them were on the verge of giggles.

Old Serendipity stepped through the gateway and peered at the brash faces before him. This nervy crew was all new to him. Bold dark eyes in faces ranging from tawny olive to deep brown, similar to those he had once been acquainted with, but this was 21st Street. A different turf—theirs. He was finding

out that moving just one block in the city could be like cross-ing a foreign border.

Willie was unable to hold back any longer. "Some loony creep things you up to, man!" he sneered. "We seen ya!" The boy, looking younger than his eleven years, bobbed out from the rear of the group, a tiny Santa Cruz medallion swinging over his sweaty, bare chest.

Hoots and giggles broke loose, the kids jostling one another in delight.

A maroon-brown girl with stringy legs skipped forward. "Seen you, Mister Weirdo, yeah!" Alma screeched, getting caught on a trailing sneaker lace.

"Gotta be loony, man—what else?" called Lucky, the youth with the ballpoint tattoos. He grimaced at the watchman from under a tangle of jet hair.

Mr. Serendipity sniffed. "Beg your pardon?" he said, un-wittingly adding fuel to their fun.

"Not for real, Mister," Otis shouted into his ear. This brought howls of glee, someone shouting, "Creepy loon!"

Willie's cousin Pequita screwed her pretty face into a scorn-ful smile. "Sneaking around in there doing nutty things."

"Hey, man—you a crazy?"

"Crazy creepy?"

"Whoo-woooo!"

"And, stinking up the place!"

"Yeah-yeah-yeah," the girls sang.

Chino tugged the bicycle chain around his neck, whirling a finger in circles alongside his temple. "Talking to goats, man. Bug-bug, man!"

"Oh wow, man," Otis added, "like if you don't know whut you doing—then somebody have to wisen you up. Right?"

"Yeah," Chino's twin, Chico, jeered. "*Us.*"

A gawky boy with his arm in a grime-stained plaster cast, threw his chest out. "Somebody got to keep this neighborhood shaped up," boomed Louie-Louie. "Dig? Like, high class re-spec-ta-ble."

"Dig it." Willie pointed about at his friends. "We got enough freaks around without *you.*"

Alma's shriek rose up above the hilarity that followed. She stood motioning at Agamemnon who had made a sudden appearance, the goat coming up alongside Mr. Serendipity. Everyone fell back, holding their noses and stumbling about, gasping exaggeratedly for air. Chico collapsed against the fence as though mortally wounded.

"Pee-yewww," he groaned. "Hey, Lou-Lou—smells worse'n that cast of yours!" The boy laughed as Louie-Louie hotly chased him down the block, his mouldering cast waving in fury overhead. With this, the game of baiting the old man lost its interest.

Casting catcalls and taunts back over their shoulders, the street kids drifted off towards the avenue, groping through their pockets to find enough change for sodas. The watchman murmured something to himself then shut the gate from the inside. "Only words, old friend, pay them no mind."

Agamemnon lowered his head and drank from a barrel of rain water. "Tell me, Ag," the old man asked in afterthought. "Do you think, well . . . that I . . . might be, you know, what they called me?" The goat ran his pink tongue across his lips.

Hmm. Seems to me, old man, most of you are.

Mr. Serendipity smiled ruefully and stepped up into the shed. He got the envelope with his paycheck which had come that morning, then left the lot. Walking uptown, he stopped at a local bank and cashed the check, then went on, proceeding east. After going crosstown two avenues, he arrived at a street that had long been part of the city's wholesale garden district—a block of squalid lofts and decrepit store fronts. Streaked and blacked-out windows hid much of the lush green worlds which filled the shops. Here was sold everything from expensive, exotic house plants the size of small trees, to flowers and vegetables, both as seed and seedlings, set in shallow flats. The old man kept his excitement at seeing it all in check, shuffling from one place to another down the street, fingering stems and looking with a wary, knowing eye at the undersides of leaves for signs of pests and blight.

He finally selected a dozen healthy tomato plants of two varieties, a number of well formed strawberry runners and some fifteen flats of vegetable sprouts. Then, unable to resist the displays of flower seeds, he ended up buying an entire bag full of seed packets though he had no idea at the time of where he would use them.

Old Serendipity's purchases filled most of the back seat of the cab he hailed. The driver watched him by way of his rear view mirror, grinning, as he saw his rider squeeze himself onto the seat amidst all his packages, propping a carton of sundries on his lap.

"So, papa, where to?" the cabbie asked.

The watchman's head poked through the greenery envelop-

ing it. "Oh. Yes. West 21st, if you don't mind. To the main gate of the . . ." He caught himself. "Er, just east of Tenth Avenue. I'll show you."

He was carried right up to his very doorstep, the cab turning onto the curbside ramp for trucks.

In the evening, after a nap, Mr. Serendipity finished planting the vegetable plot, enlarging it to hold the new seedlings he had bought. Lying between the bulldozer and a dump truck, the plot ran some fifty-by-twenty feet, ringed by stakes with wire between them.

Agamemnon looked on while the man worked into the night by the light of watch-lanterns, making no comment until the strawberry runners were set, off in a plot to themselves along the sunny side of the fence. Ag stepped into the lantern light.

Strawberries? Here?

The old man straightened; he wiped his hands on a rag. "With some luck."

And, where do you buy that?

"That?" replied the old man, absently.

Luck.

"Ahhh that. Nowhere—that is, it just comes around I suppose. By itself."

The picture postcard which showed up in the company mailbox behind a slot in the fence had a color photo of wooded hills, a rippling stream in the foreground. On the message side was a web of hand-lettered sentences, the words crooked and tightly cramped together. In time though, the message came through. Mr. Serendipity read the card aloud to Ag. " 'Dear

Hanibul,' he starts off. 'Seeing as I forgot to leave you my address I'm writing first. New York City seems long far away now. Can't tell you how good it feels to be back. The catfish were happy to see me, I figure—I got nine first time out using crickets! Yesterday I registered up for voting in the Fall. We are looking to elect one of our own for sheriff, something never done before in these parts. We can do it if everybody plus old folks get off their butts and votes! Write a few lines when you can.' " Mr. Serendipity smiled to himself and ended, " 'C. H. Mackelgum'."

It felt good to be remembered. Each time he reread the postcard he had that same warm glow come to him. Mr. Serendipity tacked it, photo side out, onto the wall over his workbench. Then he sat down. Covering both sides of a sheet of company stationery, he wrote a prompt letter in reply, addressing the envelope to a route number in Reedsboro, Maryland; a spot he was unable to locate in his United States atlas.

Except for a coke bottle which came crashing onto the shed roof, the next week was uneventful. The foreman phoned, directing him to paint *No Posting* signs along the fence and informing him that the strike was "still in negotiations" with no end in sight yet. The picket patrol had now dwindled to two men with signs who arrived to march for only three hours each morning; the shutdown was a clear success and did not require more effort than that to keep it that way.

With nothing but time on his hands, old Serendipity seeded a patch of clover for Ag, and got the squash vines curling their way up a grid of framing at the foot of the steelwork. He decided to start all the new flower seeds in a number of large

shallow troughs used for mixing cement, placing three different annuals into a thick bed of river-silt. He then covered the troughs with sheets of translucent builders' plastic, a roll of which he found in a toolbin. Couldn't have better for light and holding moisture, he told himself.

Under the steady care he gave them, the garden plots thrived. The weather was ideal now for growing things. And, by the first day of June, the strawberry plants had doubled in size on their wooden supports and they soon flowered.

·THE KIDS·

In the afternoons, when school let out for the day, West 21ST was a field for street games and arguments, some of which flared into scraps that died away quickly. Mixing with the name-calls were the cries of the scraped-ices vendor and the *cuchifritos* man as they traveled the block with their homemade carts.

Chino treated all the guys on his team to *cuchies*—spicy, tri-cornered dumplings stuffed with chopped meat and fried in deep fat—the day he slammed three triples in one stickball game, wiping out the other side.

That same week, Louie-Louie took over the unofficial skelly championship, by beating Hands in a three-out-of-five series. Their knuckles blackened and raw from the asphalt roadbed,

the pair had fought to a tie, two games even. Then Louie-Louie called "time." Racing upstairs he scrounged through drawers and found his ace-shooter. He repacked the bottle cap with melted wax, adding a penny for weight, and returned to the chalk-lined field of boxes which numbered 1 to 9. With new confidence, he finger-flicked his shooter from box to box, knocking Hands' bottle cap yards out of the field.

Willie was all smiles these days—brother Ramon had come home from the army. In one piece.

Willie was so happy he shocked his old man by *offering* to tend to his father's pigeon coop on the roof of their tenement. He got out of bed to do it when his father left for his job at the handbag factory. At 7 A.M. Willie would climb the stairs to the fifth floor, then, breathing through his mouth only, he would sweep out the big pigeon coop of wood and chicken wire, then fill the bird troughs with feed. In the hour before dusk, standing fearlessly alongside Ramon on the parapet wall overlooking the street, Willie would circle a long bamboo pole in the air, making cooing sounds until the flock returned for the night to their shelves inside the coop.

His cousin, Pequita, was now old enough to help her widowed godmother afternoons in her *bodega*. This tiny grocery and general neighborhood store next to the barbershop on Ninth Avenue was hung with curls of gluey flypaper. Religious plaques covered one wall and a päpier-maché saint stood guard over the cash register. On humid days the combined aromas of garlic, incense, green bananas and saffron which rose up from the store was enough to drive Lucky from the room overhead which he shared with his two younger brothers. The smells

gave him one more excuse to stay out in the street perfecting his skill at top-spinning. It was Lucky's passion for tops which led to his nickname two summers earlier when he was eleven.

He had been spinning two tops at a time when, jumping a crack in the pavement, his torpedo landed in an empty lot, disappearing into the rubbish and weeds. Searching for over an hour he never found it. But he found something else instead—a rotting paper bag under a mattress. Inside it was another bag, and inside that another one of plastic. And lastly, wrapped in some newspaper, $240.00. In twenties. Lucky might never have turned the money in, but with a patrol car driving by at the moment, he had no choice. At the precinct station house, the desk sergeant said his find was likely "numbers dough"—collection money from the illegal lottery run by racketeers in poor neighborhoods around the city. The cop proved to be right; at least no one ever showed up to claim the money. So Lucky became the first kid on the block with a bank account, and got himself a new name.

On days when her mom worked as a maid for families crosstown on the rich upper East Side, Alma sometimes had to baby-sit with her little sister, Doreen, if one of the neighbors couldn't look after her. Usually she would take her over to the schoolyard on 18th where the four-year-old could run free and Alma could watch Otis shoot baskets—"his all-the-time bag"—when he wasn't hitching rides on busses or over at the river with Malcolm, his best buddy.

There was always something doing down there. You might pick up some things; small articles dropped in loading and unloading the freighters. But the *bossest* time was after it rained.

When the river rats were still holed-up in their burrows. The trick was to hold burning rolls of newspaper at all of their tunnel exits except one, while armed with rocks and bats, everyone stood ready for the mad squealing dash into the air that would follow.

In most things the twins, Chico and Chino, worked together as a team. They had worked out a cool system for the route they covered of the subway gratings at bus stops along Eighth Avenue. Their thing was fishing for lost money. Of course there was competition from others, kids from elsewhere who came to drop their lines hung with chewing gum-tipped lead sinkers through spaces in the sidewalk gratings. Most would soften the gum first with a match flame, which was hip. But the twins who would fish up as much as a dollar and a half on good days were doing even better lately. High John, the neighborhood blindman, had recommended they dip the sinkers into thick varnish. This worked so well that the pair bought the shabby vagrant a handful of cigars in appreciation, his lifeless eyes flickering wide with surprise.

When June days grew steamy, even the best of street games could become a drag. This was when everybody thought of water. For decades the Hudson had been too polluted to swim in. There were always the hydrants, if the cops felt lenient, and if the older guys didn't have a stickball game going in the road.

One day the kids tried the public pool way downtown. It was mobbed as ever. By the time they paid their quarter admission, the chlorinated water was lukewarm. Still it was better than nothing. They felt refreshed afterwards—until the airless subway ride home. By the time they arrived on the block

again, damp towels rolled under their arms, they were feeling hot and clammy once more.

Louie-Louie squinted up at a *toro* that skipped through the haze overhead. "Man," he panted. "Wish I was tied to a string. Fly, man, fly."

"Yeah. Right on," Otis agreed. "Then just cut the string, man, and take off, *shoomdeedo*."

"To where, Otis man?" Alma said, teasing. She tugged at her little sister's hand as Doreen tried to keep step.

Otis looked outward. "I don't know, just anywheres but here."

Several heads bobbed in agreement. "I wish I was Superman," Hands murmured.

"Me—I'll take P.R., man," Willie said dreamily. "My uncle says the water's all blue and green down Puerto Rico."

"With palm trees and banana trees all over, mm," Pequita sighed.

Louie-Louie spotted the old creep first. Waggling his plaster encased forearm, he pointed ahead toward the construction fence. The kids began a wail of whinnies and brays, mimicking what they thought to be a barnyard. Pequita came to a stop a pace from the old man who stood over a bucket of blue paint, a wet brush in his hand.

She curtsied. "Hel . . . lo, Mister Creepsie," Pequita hissed in a honey-sweet voice. Her grin brought forth a chorus of hoots.

"Hello, miss," the watchman replied, dipping his brush. He painted a foot-high letter N on the fence.

Willie eyed it and loosed a guffaw. "Oh, wow! Like N, for Nuts!"

"Right, right!" Malcolm called.

The watchman remained quiet, now completing a letter O.

"O for . . . for . . ." Alma paused to pin down her thought.

"*Outasight*, baby!" Otis crowed. "Like this kook here."

"Outa his skull!" Willie jeered, the others giggling.

Alma and Pequita began to dance around Mr. Serendipity, the boys beating out a rhythm with their hand claps and chanting, "Loony-loony-*uh!* Loony-loony-*uh!* . . ."

Without glancing to either side of him, old Serendipity drew the first letter of a second word, P.

Louie-Louie leaned in and examined it. "Beautiful. Dig it—P for Putrid, man! The way that goat and him stink!"

The old man shucked his head and seemed to smile to himself. He put the brush down atop the bucket. "Some of you are right good with words," he said calmly. "Now, this young fellow for example—sorry, lad, I don't know your name." He stood looking to Louie-Louie for a response; there was none.

The boys fell silent, suspicious that he was baiting a trap of some kind.

"Louie-Louie," piped a small voice from the rear.

Alma spun round at her sister Doreen. "Shush up, brat!"

"Yeah, Doreen," Willie said melodramatically in a hushed voice. "Gotta watch these old creeps—anybody see that movie on TV once where there was this weird old guy . . . ?"

"Interesting name—Louie-Louie," said Mr. Serendipity. "Two names, is it?"

"Nah—they only call me that," Louie-Louie said before he knew it.

Doreen stepped forward, and stood looking down at the can of blue paint. "I don't know spelling words yet," she mumbled. "But I'm good making pictures."

Alma swooped, poking her to be still, others cawing at the four-year-old traitor to their cause.

"Would you care to try painting one?" The old man handed her the brush. He pointed to the fence. "Lots of space."

Before Alma could get a hold on her wrist Doreen had slipped out of reach and began a heavy blue scrawl on the fence with the brush.

Mr. Serendipity smiled, asking, "Anyone else? It's a long fence."

A fast huddle between three of the boys took place. After some buzzing among them, Willie came over, a blank look masking his intentions.

"Got another one, man?" he asked.

Old Serendipity was startled for a second, then he beamed. "Yes, yes . . ." he called, rushing off through the open gate. "Back in a minute."

Stirring out of a nap under the shed porch, Ag saw the man go to a locker, rummage about within, come up with a paint brush then run out to the boardwalk again.

"Here we are!" he announced. He blinked seeing Willie sputter and break into a howl of laughter. Their fingers pointing at the fence behind him, the kids broke into gleeful jeers. The watchman turned stiffly and saw the ten-foot-long slogan now emblazoned across the wooden panels:

THE WORLD'S BIGGEST WEIRDO LIVES HERE!!!

Mr. Serendipity looked on unperturbed, or so it seemed. He felt a nip at his shirt sleeve and saw Doreen waving a blue-smeared hand up at him.

"Like," she began, pointing at her drawing, "is that the— the way a goat looks?"

The others drowned out her last words with whoops and hollers. Squinting at the boldly painted picture, the watchman put on his glasses.

"Hmm . . . Agamemnon might not agree," he said. "But I'd say it does . . ."

"Doreen," the little girl filled in.

"*Brat!*" Alma snapped, turning her sister towards the curb and marching her off.

.TRUCE.

Another hail of beer cans came over the 21st Street fence followed by taunts and the sounds of escaping feet. Later that afternoon the watchman noticed Willie, Pequita and Lucky huddled together outside the gate. Pretending not to see, he edged closer to them, working a hoe among the vegetables as he went.

Willie watched him through the opening in the gate. "Can't grow stuff in that junk," he scoffed.

Lucky let a top fly onto the boardwalk.

"Looks like," Pequita said, "he's doing pretty okay."

"And what d'you know about it, anyhow?" Lucky muttered.

Willie shrugged. "From my uncle . . ."

"What's he know, man?" the older boy shot back. "These ain't bananas, besides he's from San Juan, not the country part." Lucky squatted down and slipped his flattened palm under the top, bringing it, still spinning, up with him as he straightened.

Willie bristled. "Knows more'n you, dude," he said hoarsely.

Lucky grinned, then jutted his chin towards the lot. "Some boss machines in there, huh?"

The trio pressed up to the fence peering through gaps in it at the spread of abandoned machines; the bulldozer, derricks and trucks frozen in positions in which they had been left weeks before. Willie stiffened abruptly and elbowed Lucky. The big gate had opened, and the old guy stood there.

"Quite right," he said to Lucky, "bananas would never grow here at all—but strawberries can. Wasn't sure when I put them in, but only this morning I saw the first little green ones."

Bananas? Little green ones? He's really freaked out, the boys thought as they stared back coldly.

"Strawberries?" Pequita mumbled.

Mr. Serendipity nodded cheerily, suggesting they come inside and have a look for themselves. Otis came trotting from across the street, a cracked broomstick in his hands.

"Send that billy goat to the meat factory?" he hooted. "Like, I don't smell him around, man." Otis snickered, the others joining him, except for Pequita, who had walked ahead and now stood a pace inside the lot, looking about.

"Guess the wind's blowing the wrong way," the old man said. "Actually, you can find Ag over behind that bulldozer

somewhere; he's not always cheerful, but he is gentle." Mr. Serendipity ambled back through the gateway.

The boys exchanged amused looks and whispered something to one another. Willie left them, saying with a smirk he had better things to do.

Moving stiffly, her eyes swiveling warily as if she had entered a cemetery at night, Pequita trailed after the watchman between the garden plots. "They sort of spruce up the place, don't you think?" he said. Pequita made no reply; they went on. The watchman pointed out the line of cement troughs. "All under those plastic sheets are new seedlings, flowers."

"Now, here," he said and grinned proudly, "these are the strawberries."

He led the girl over to the patch of bushy plants which stood before the fence. She gazed at them for a moment, then bent over and fingered some berries; tiny and still yellowish-green, they were the size of peas.

"These," she breathed, "really going to be . . ."

"If everything goes well they should be ripe for picking inside of ten days, I think."

A murmur of surprise came from the girl; her eyes ran from plant to plant. "You put in, I mean like seeds, and got these?"

Mr. Serendipity shook his head. "Takes too long to start them from seed; these came from runners." Then, seeing her puzzlement, he knelt down and pointed to one of the green tendrils which grew outward from the base of the nearest vine. "Runners," he said, "are cut from the best of mature plants then rooted in a special way to make growing stock for new plants."

"Hey!" They looked up at the call which had come from the steelwork. "Hey mister! What's he eat?" Otis and Lucky were seen standing alongside Ag in the distance.

"Most anything, when he's hungry enough!" the watchman called back.

Pequita knelt down beside him. "What'd you mean before when you said 'if everything goes well'?"

His fingers reached for and picked a mealy bug off a leaf where it had been feeding. "Oh," he said, "soil and weather conditions, you know, and keeping blights and bugs like this one from doing damage."

The old man nodded to himself. "Plants are living things . . ." He spoke on for several minutes, telling about root systems and how they develop, and describing the marvelous ways in which plants use sunlight, water and foods from the soil. So delighted was he to find a curious listener, especially a young person, the information just rolled from him: so much was stored inside him which had gone unshared during his solitary years. With barely a pause he rattled on, facts tumbling from him at a rather bewildering rate. Pequita's black eyes fluttered, squinted, and at times opened wide, as she tried to follow his words. Finally, laughing at himself for running on so, Mr. Serendipity asked the girl to wait and hurried into the shed.

He returned with a thick volume in his hand, his best botany text. Pequita turned the pages and scanned the numerous diagrams and detailed illustrations.

Otis and Lucky had since discovered that a bulldozer could become a spaceship. Now, noisily manning the array of frozen controls up in the cockpit, the boys were defending themselves

against an attack from some awesome enemy—Martians, from the sound of things.

It doesn't take long for word to spread to the kids of West 21st. By five, the rest of the machines were filled with youngsters, several squeezed into each of the cab seats. Willie scoffed that they were suckers for going, and he went down to the river to scale stones at the pier when Hands and Louie-Louie left for the lot.

The twins drifted over and joined the watchman as he and Pequita toured the garden plots. Mr. Serendipity was still talking away, pointing out everything he thought might be of interest.

All the while the sound effects of battle filled the air, the derricks now attacking the bulldozer and trucks. It was a wonder that anyone heard the supper calls when they came from windows across the way.

"I think," piped Doreen, "Mom's calling."

"Um . . ." murmured Alma, ducking the rockets which whizzed by their cab window up in the derrick. She felt a poke from her sister. "Yeah, okay . . . go on, Dorie," she said in her nicest big-sister voice. "Tell Mom I'll be five minutes."

Doreen waggled her head. "Uh uh."

"Now, c'mon, Dorie hon', go on."

The little one's pout tightened, her spindly arms folded across the stripes of her T-shirt.

Alma's eyes flashed. "You go on, brat—or you don't get to come here tomorrow!"

That did it. Scrambling to the ground, pout and all, the four-year-old ran off like a shot.

From that day on, any worries old Serendipity might still have had about attacks on his garden could be put to rest.

They would arrive right after school, books under their arms, and on weekends, in the late mornings. Mr. Serendipity usually greeted the early comers at the gate, Ag at his side, peering out from behind him.

It's not the gardens they come for, old man.

Old Serendipity got this comment from Agamemnon after the kids' second visit. He laughed; it didn't matter to him why. He had overheard Otis crack that flowers were "jive stuff for girls."

It was only Pequita at first, and at times Chico and Chino, who lent the watchman a hand, helping to water and fertilize the planting areas. For the others, what were flowers compared with a bulldozer which could be turned into a submarine one moment and a spaceship the next, with the remarkable flexibility of diving fifty fathoms into the sea then blasting off into the cosmos? "Power, man, pour it on!" Otis was heard commanding.

Street kids, after all, were born and raised in a world of tired brick and asphalt, knowing much more from TV about the moon than about growing things. To them, greenery meant a park. If you could get to one. Flowers—these were things you glimpsed in shop windows, or the waxy plastic kind your old lady got at the five-and-dime and kept on top of the TV set.

It was the strawberries becoming full and ripe that brought about the change. A big one.

"Oh, wow!" Louie-Louie breathed when he picked a huge berry off and held it before his eyes.

"Big as a Torpedo," Lucky said, holding a top alongside the luscious-looking strawberry; a small exaggeration that everyone agreed with.

"You made, I mean, grew these just from the ground like?" Louie-Louie asked.

"From runners," replied Pequita, looking to the old man for confirmation.

"That's right. Here." He handed the youth a plastic bucket and motioned toward the strawberry patch. "Why don't we have some?"

There was no need to make the suggestion again. Chico found a small empty carton, and among them, the kids picked enough of the fruit for a feast. They washed the berries under a standpipe tap that was outside the shed. Then, sitting cross-legged or lying sprawled in the shade of the steelwork, they gorged themselves. Mr. Serendipity had his strawberries with milk in a bowl, offering the same to anyone who would try them this way.

Otis wagged his head, a trickle of sweet juice curling down the side of his chin. "I like 'em better straight."

"Yeah," Hands admitted after popping his twentieth into his mouth. "Something else. You pretty cool, mister. That's for sure!"

Mr. Serendipity stretched his legs, settling back against a pillar and loosening his belt a notch. He wasn't entirely sure what the boy had meant, but knew it was all right. The outside world felt very nice to be in.

In the evening after they had left, he wrote Mr. Mackelgum a long letter in which he told about the garden and about his daily visitors. How pleasant the days had now become, "thanks to you, C. H." Later, swaying idly in his hammock outside, he looked over the construction site. His eyes came to rest on the line of large mixing troughs filled with young annuals, rank upon rank of tender green seedlings which were beginning to crowd into a tangle of foliage. Nasturtium, marigold, zinnia, cornflower, petunia, portulaca, four kinds of daisy . . . so many different varieties, he couldn't recall all he had bought and put in. Hundreds, maybe thousands of sprouts, he thought, with a foolish grin. Sitting up in the hammock, he swung his legs to the ground and taking up a watch-lantern, he walked over to the troughs with Ag at his heels.

Now what are you up to, old man?

"Up to . . . ?"

Up to—up to. There's a million of them. You must have some scheme in mind. I know you.

"Well," Mr. Serendipity said, a smile flickering privately. Bending, he examined a row of double nasturtiums. "No scheme, not just yet. I expect something will come to me, though. Have to give it some thought, don't you know? Can't rush into important matters without some careful thinking."

Spending all that money without any idea of what to do with them—fine! They can't stay that way forever.

"Isn't that odd, old friend," the watchman said. "Just what I was thinking."

Brushing a hand along a thicket of shoots, he saw that they were getting leggy, their lower leaves rank and yellow from the crowded conditions in the seedling bed. He made a small sucking sound through his dentures.

Got you a problem, huh?

"If you want to look at it that way." He finished passing his lantern over the trough then checked the time clock at his waist. "Then again, how can you get an answer without one? And maybe the bigger the problem, the more interesting the answer. I think you have to sort of just let things turn free in your mind, consider them from all sides and top to bottom."

He peered into the gathering darkness. Ag pawed at the ground.

Consider long enough, and you're going to have a whole lot of dead plants on your hands.

Mr. Serendipity threw a switch on the side of the shed wall, and a host of small electric lights went on within the nine floors of the construction. His gaze traveling slowly up the steelwork, the watchman lit his pipe. I wonder . . . what would C.H. do with them?

·VOLUNTEERS·

Two hundred and ninety miles south, Reedsboro sat among the Maryland hills just past the fork of a beaten clay and gravel road. It was barely a village; one that did not appear on any gas station map.

While their settings were far different, all the jobs of growing—watering, weeding, spraying and fertilizing—were done pretty much the same way. Mr. Mackelgum worked his fourteen acre dirt-farm on a bigger scale, beginning at sunrise. But then, Mr. Serendipity would still be puttering about his garden plots until late at night, often saying a few words to his plants in the small hours. C.H. had the help of his son-in-law and a pair of bony, sway-backed mules, while old Serendipity had the aid

of some eager but inexperienced youngsters, and Ag, for whatever that was worth.

The construction strike entered its sixth week.

Ever since the strawberry feast, the watchman began to find
himself with one or more new assistants in the garden, every
other day, offering to "help, sort of." Now that school was
over for the summer, they started coming in the mornings.

Three days after the doctor cut away his cast, Louie-Louie
volunteered himself and his mended arm, taking up a wheelbarrow with Hands and spreading a load of fertilizer among
the vegetables. Along with everything else, these too were
flourishing, leafing up and outwards. The first tiny pods had
appeared under the grayish-green foliage of the bean plants.

Coming upon Alma and Otis one day, Mr. Serendipity noticed the boy sitting on his haunches and staring fixedly at the
beans. Alma glanced up at the old man, cupping a hand over a
giggle and pointing at her boyfriend.

"Ask him what he's doing," she bubbled. "Ask him, Mister
Serendip."

Otis brushed her arm down, glaring. "Just take care of your
own business, will you, girl?"

"Watching—that's what," she burst out. "Watching to see
one of them grow out!"

"No, I ain't!" Otis hissed.

"He is too—why you told me so yourself, Otis Clearwater."
Alma laughed, moving to a safer distance. "Wants to see one
of them bean pods the minute it shows up." She waggled a
finger. "Fess up to the man, go on!"

Otis arose and, fuming, grabbed his rake from the ground and stalked off, promising that he would get even with her. "Just don't let me catch you later—hear me, girl?" A couple of the other boys who were watering the cucumbers, whistled, Malcolm laughing and aiming the hose spray at him. "Be cool now, broth . . ."

It was always a laugh teasing Otis, but Alma would have been the first to admit that the way things happened among the plants was a mystery. Weird. Getting there in the morning to find entire layers of new growth in the carrot patch. Or finding another foot of squash vines twisting their way up the footing of the steelwork, or lifting some leaves and seeing baby tomatoes where you could swear none had been the day before. The others also had one or another experience like these, feeling a buzz of awe inside. Somehow, *their* hands and fingers had something to do with the changes that were taking place.

There were moments, as those when the kids rested in the shade having sodas and *cuchies*, that the old man would detect this sense of wonder in their voices.

"Actually," he revealed, "the more I'm at it, and the more I learn about growing things, the more amazing I find it all."

Whenever his helpers asked questions he would hasten to bring out his botany books. Then, his knobby, veined hands turning the pages, he would display the colored illustrations and speak of the life-cycles they showed—from seed to flower to fruit. The pictures of bugs and other pests which fed on plants fascinated his listeners; they were concerned, asking what could be done to defeat them. It was always the *how* that interested the kids: How does this happen? How you do this or

that? Once when he used the word *hybrid* a few times, Mr. Serendipity was put to the test, explaining the process of breeding new characteristics in plants. For the better part of an hour he described how carefully selected flowers of the same variety are cross-pollinated, thus creating hybrids of different sizes and colors. And similarly, how fruit or vegetable plants are crossed with one another to produce special variations of form and taste, hardiness, and even shape.

"Y'know nectarines?" Hands said out of nowhere, as he and Willie sat on his fire escape one warm evening.

Willie grunted, and sailed a folded-paper plane out over the street. "So nectarines, so peaches. So what?" Not him; he wasn't having any part of that.

"So, man—they *ain't* peaches," Hands declared triumphantly. He blew the wad of gum from his mouth. "They come from mixing peaches with plums."

"Big deal, man," Willie jeered. "So somebody goes and marries a coupla fruits together. Big deal."

Lost in thought, Hands kept looking down the block towards the construction off Tenth. "Those things he's got growing over there," he said quietly. "Like . . . they're living things."

Willie squinted and looked into his friend's face, then wagged his head sadly. "Oh . . . maaaan. You getting psycho as the old creep."

It took place naturally, in the course of events. Working in the garden made it all more and more real, and before long it began to be an important part of their lives.

Louie-Louie and Alma liked tending the vegetables best.

They kept the rows free of weeds as soon as weeds emerged, and watered them in a new way they'd learned, letting a hose trickle slowly along the shallow trenches between the plants. Hands and Malcolm devoted a lot of time to the tomatoes which now were bowing with young glistening fruit.

"Be needing bigger stakes soon," Malcolm said to his partner.

Hands agreed. "I know where we can cop us a bunch of mop and broom handles."

"Yeah, they'd be good."

Pequita and a friend, Lena, adopted the flower beds as theirs to care for. The marigolds and petunias were brilliant and the zinnias were giant in size and of every hue.

Chico and his twin Chino, along with Lucky, took over the squash plants, the boys admiring the way the vines wove higher up the framing of the steelwork each day as if determined not to let any obstacle get in their way. The vines had reached past the first landing. Old Serendipity showed them how to vapor spray them against the heat. And on sultry days, Chico, a hose line slung over his shoulder, would climb the framing to cool off the topmost leaves—something he could have done from the ground or a ladder, but what risk was there in doing it the easy way?

Little Doreen took the job she gave herself very seriously. Roving the plots, she was ever on the lookout for worms, aphids or Japanese beetles at work on the underside of leaves. "B—Bugs!" she'd shriek the instant she spotted anything suspicious.

As the kids gardened, an almost steady banter went back and forth between them, sly put-downs mostly. Ag came in for

his share—no one was immune. But if it bothered him, he didn't show it; the clover patch he had all to himself was doing nicely.

Towards the end of June, Otis began to notice the watchman hovering over the big mixing troughs thick with flower seedlings, an odd look playing over his face—a worried look, the boy thought. He watched Mr. Serendipity. The old man paced to and fro repeatedly looking from the seedling beds to various places about the lot. After some minutes of this, Otis silently signaled to Malcolm and some of the others, motioning toward the watchman with his head. They saw him clamp tighter on the unlit pipe in his mouth, shade his eyes, gaze up at the steel-work, then wag his head no. Again he began his pacing, now mumbling something under his breath.

"Say something, Mister Serendip?" Louie-Louie finally asked, unable to contain himself any longer.

Mr. Serendipity caught himself. "Huh? Oh."

"Something wrong?" Otis asked.

The old man came over. "No, not exactly," he said, his eyes going back to the troughs, lingering there.

"Yeah," Otis said. "Must be a million of them you got there."

Hands scratched his cheek. "Where you figger on putting them all? They ain't growing anymore, all tangled like that."

Alma joined the group and peered about. "We need a lot of space, I mean, to transplant all that . . ." She could see that those areas of the lot not already planted were occupied by mounded gravel, sand and supplies or taken up with machinery and deep pits.

"Oh," said the watchman, "I suppose we could clear over at

that end and fill the pits." They saw him indicate the Tenth Avenue section of the fence. "But . . ." He paused. "That wouldn't be very . . . interesting, would it?"

Interesting? The word echoed within his listeners.

"Interesting?" Hands said somewhat impatiently. "Man, if they're not transplanted soon, they've had it. Right? Didn't you tell us that once about seedlings?"

Old Serendipity nodded firmly.

"So why don't we just *do* it?" Alma said, walking over to him. She picked up a spade to show her readiness to begin.

Otis and Lucky stood over one of the troughs. "A whole lot of skinny looking things here, man," Otis said. A murmur of concern ran through the group.

Mr. Serendipity said he had to confess that he had been delaying transplanting the seedlings. "You see," he confided, plucking at his beard, "I thought something special ought to be done with these flowers; there are so many and so many kinds. Look here." He passed along the troughs.

"Daisies . . . four kinds, including shastas. Portulaca over here, nasturtium and cornflowers . . ." His voice and gestures grew more excited as he went on, reciting the names of another dozen annuals. "Imagine." He stopped and turned to the group. "All of them in bloom together. Imagine!"

As he searched for the words to exactly mirror his feelings, his eyes looked wild. No one had ever seen him this way before. "One glorious sea of flowering color. Can you *see* it?"

Mr. Serendipity said the last in a tone of such low intensity some of the kids thought that the sun was affecting him. Standing before them his arms wide, a breeze flapping his baggy

workpants and a button missing from the shirt over his paunch, he looked comical, almost ridiculous.

No one said anything. The group glanced at one another in embarrassment for him. *Psycho*: Lucky thought of Willie's word for the old man.

"Now, then," Mr. Serendipity said with a clap of his hands. "Why hide so much loveliness behind a fence?" He swept his hand in an arc. "Those are awfully gray looking streets past the fence I said to myself just last night."

"Wigged—wigged way out," Chico whispered into Chino's ear. "Maybe we was right about him in the first place."

Chino hated to, but had to admit it. "Like a bedbug," he breathed back out of the side of his mouth.

"I also asked myself," the watchman went on, as if debating, "why do they have to be confined to growing only on the ground?" He took pause to look at the group.

"You asked yourself *that*, huh?" Otis said, his tone suggesting that he thought the old guy wasn't well.

"I did." Old Serendipity nodded, adding, "of course, that's their rightful place in the countryside—in fields and meadows, on hillsides, but . . ." He drew a breath. "*This* is the city, isn't it?"

Baffled expressions were exchanged, Lucky finally breaking the silence.

"Dig it, you stupes?" he shouted suddenly. "Up! In the city everything goes up! The man means we plant 'em up *there!*" Eleven sets of eyes widened in disbelief as they followed the line of Lucky's finger which pointed directly up at the steelwork.

"It's only sitting around getty rusty," the watchman said quietly.

"Oh, wow," someone said hoarsely.

"Zow-ie!"

"Dynamite!"

A pell-mell chorus of shouts and laughter came from the street kids. Agamemnon watched them prance about, jostling and bumping one another, giddy at the notion. The old man stood in their midst, beaming.

That evening when his young visitors filed out the gate, they were chattering with anticipation.

"It could really be something, wouldn't you say?" Mr. Serendipity asked after everyone had left. "Long lines of flowers fluttering above the street?" He stopped. "Hmm. Think it's a pretty fool notion, eh Ag?"

Did I say that, old man?

"You don't have to. It's written all over your face, old friend," he said, thinking of the kids' gleeful response. "Well, *they* take to the idea even if you don't. But, that's all right—can't expect everyone to understand."

Ag tossed his head. *Go on, keep putting words into my mouth if it pleases you.*

Later, when the supper dishes were washed and put away, the watchman finished a letter to C.H. He'd go for the idea, thought Mr. Serendipity as he sealed the envelope.

He went outside and walked over to the work lift, entered the cage, then threw the lever. The lift creaked and began to rise. The old man could hardly wait for daylight.

· WILLIE ·

Willie, the loner, heard the latest from a couple of the guys. "Yeah," he scoffed to himself, "they putting me on."

He moved easily along the roof ledge overlooking the street, watching his brother Ramon calling in their flock with circles of the bamboo signal pole. A successful raid on some downtown flock was being concluded. Among the flapping sun-rimmed pigeons now arriving could be seen a pair of strangers.

"Two, baby!" Ramon announced to the world. "Two, *mira*—see them? Right this way—*casa mio*—come to papa my pretty-pretties!"

Willie laughed, looking admiringly at Ramon. He saw him bow low and, with a grand flourish of his free hand, wave the

birds in, several of them landing on the tar paper of the coop.

"That's it—right this way dum-dums!" Willie sang as the flock female cooed into a softly whirring landing, the two male pigeons that she had lured astray right behind her. "Follow the cute li'l chick."

The boy jumped from the wall and swiftly opened the door to the coop, then waiting until the two strangers strutted inside after the lead dove, he snapped it shut.

Willie did some fast figuring, adding up the males they'd taken to date and subtracting those kidnapped from them by other flocks from neighborhoods as far downtown as Houston Street.

"Six, Ramon," he called, giving the tally. They were way ahead. "Not counting the one the cat grabbed, we're six up on those downtown jokers!"

And here June had barely ended; at this rate their summer bag of strays would easily exceed last year's raids. His eyes gleaming like onyx, Willie looked over the pigeons coming to rest all about the corner of the roof. Starting with the pair of racers his father had brought home four years ago, their flock now numbered forty-two; some twenty of which were captive strays.

The boy's gaze came to an abrupt halt . . . in line with the construction site diagonally away and down the block. Hey! the thing, the work lift, was running again. He quickly filled the feed trays then went loping downstairs and over to the lot.

No two ways about it, something was sure going on.

Its motor droning, cables squealing over pulleys, the lift was making a slow trip up the steelwork. Willie stood in the gate-

way, one thumb hooked in his garrison belt, and looked on. So the guys hadn't been jiving him. He saw the lift come to a stop on the fourth landing. Yeah, there was the old kook. He saw the figure of the watchman wave breezily down to his crew of assistants working on the ground, then open the lift door. As the old man began to carry a series of bushel baskets from the cage, the wind shifted, bringing the swampy odor of river silt at Willie. The boy knuckled his nose. "Oh, maaan," he groaned.

A raucous laugh came from nearby. Willie turned and saw one of his closest pals, Jojo, lower a wheelbarrow to rest. "You get used to it, —our secret weapon, man. Can you dig it?"

"It could wipe out the neighborhood," Willie snorted.

"It sure does the job," Jojo shot back, lifting the wheelbarrow arms. "Just take a look around, broth."

Willie fell into step with the other boy, masking his curiosity with a super-cool look, his finger still in his belt, eyes half-lidded towards the ground. "Secret weapon . . ." he said, as if he couldn't care less.

But Jojo knew the cool-game too. "Like I said—secret," he murmured back, refusing to be drawn out. He veered off with the wheelbarrow. "No time to rap, man, got too much to do."

Willie watched him go off towards Hands and Malcolm who stood in the distance, spading earth into bushel baskets. Adopting as bored an expression as he could muster, he sauntered across the lot, passing between the vegetable and flower plots. Slowly, taking things in out of the corner of his eye, he became aware of the radiance of all that was blooming about him. The boy paused over a zinnia bigger than his open hand.

Nice to have a shirt that color, he thought, then catching himself—*flowers!* What kind of trick has the creep got them guys suckered into? He studied the sight of his friends moving about the steelwork beyond.

Malcolm and Hands kept filling wheelbarrows with earth as fast as Louie-Louie and Jojo could cart them away. At the lift door were Alma and Lucky, shoveling the earth into baskets which, in turn, Chino carried inside the lift cage. When the lift was loaded, Chico would start the winch motor, at the same moment sending a two-finger whistle into the air, signaling its ascent to the watchman high above.

He whistles pretty good, Willie had to admit. He saw the lift move upwards to where the old man eagerly awaited it, shovel in hand.

Humming a strain of *Funiculi-Funicula*, the watchman went along the south side of the platform, spading out the new load of soil. They had decided to plant the sunny side of the steelwork facing 21st Street. The plan was to fill all the yards of open channel which ran along the outer edge of each floor—the channel designed and built to hold water pipe and electrical cable one day. "Just about perfect for flower boxes," Mr. Serendipity had pointed out. The plan so fired everyone's imagination the work was proceeding very quickly; three floors a day were being planted with seedlings.

By the weekend, the watchman was working along the sixth floor I-beams, his suntan turning bronze now. He made his way along the leading edge of the steelwork showing as little concern for the height as the toro flyers on their rooftop perches.

He chose the cooler hours after sundown for the more

delicate job of transplanting the tender flower sprouts into the earth-filled channels. Setting each into place individually, he would tamp the topping of river silt about the roots with his gloved finger tips, then sprinkle each line from a watering can. The watchman had to insist he alone do all work which took place up in the construction itself, fearful about the risk to his helpers if they joined him. There was quite a bit of grumbling about this at the outset, but the kids finally agreed.

Although the work was demanding, harder than any the old man had done before, he never faltered, looking to each day with renewed vigor, feeling no aches in his bones. Not even a twinge of "the rheumatiz," he realized.

"Though, I suppose," he confided to Ag upon awakening one day, "this might be due to the dry spell we're having." He peered at the sky through a window; still no sign of rain. "We could use a good shower about now. Unusual for New York to go so long this way."

Not for Serbia.

The old man sat up. "Now how would you know that? It's your ancestors that were born there, not you." He chuckled at Agamemnon emerging from under the kitchen table.

Point-zero-five inches of rainfall in the mountains. Remember, old man? You read me about the place from one of those fat books.

The old man smiled; he had indeed, he recalled. One wintry evening long ago, in the basement below the twin-tenements. But all that seemed so far away now with all that had since taken place.

"My, my, how quickly things go past," he mused, getting his slippers on and going to the sink. "Almost like a dream, don't you know?" Ag had nothing more to say. Nosing the shed door open, the goat went down the porch steps. The youngsters could be heard arriving, their voices a welcome sound in the sunlight.

Willie showed up for the second day running.

"Forget it, man," he said, letting everyone know promptly that he was only there killing some time—not about to take part in anything. He drifted across the lot, looking on as his friends put their assembly line into motion once more: earth and silt spaded into wheelbarrows, on into the bushel baskets, Chico's piercing whistle, then the lift rising.

Pequita and Lena were transferring the seedlings from the beds in the cement troughs into a set of shallow fruit crates scrounged up from local vegetable markets.

Willie sidled over to where Jojo was rolling a huge empty oil drum over to the work lift door.

"Hey, Jojo," he said, after watching him for a bit. "That." He pointed at the drum. "For what, man?"

Jojo brushed him off with a wave and opened the cage. "C'mon, man," he grimaced as Willie kept on his heels. "What difference to you, if I told you—for what? Off my back, man." The youth tipped the oil drum back and rolled it onto the lift.

"Okay for you, pal." Willie brayed, shrugging and turning away only to turn back sharply again. "Who was it, huh, that sneaked you into the movies last week. Huh?" He fixed Jojo with a squint of accusation. It was Willie who had gotten the fire exit open using a wire coat hanger, getting the four

of them into the theater before the usher knew what was happening. This was a debt of a high order around West 21st.

Louie-Louie came past them. "The picture stunk," he said with chilling finality, and set down a crate full of seedlings in the lift.

"Right—he's right Willie-man," Jojo said.

"Oh, yeah?"

"Yeah," Louie-Louie said.

"Yeah," Jojo echoed.

Willie kicked a clump of earth loose and got into a deeper slouch.

"So how was *I* supposed to know, you guys?" he mumbled. Then he broke into a grin. "Didn't the sign outside say it was 'Rated X'—like it was you cats who were so *sure* the picture was a winner—right?"

He had them there. "Okay, dum-dum," Jojo said, "seeing as you're so ignorant—this drum here is for water. Dig." He stepped out of the steelwork's shadow and gestured upwards.

A curve of green plastic hose line could be seen running up the construction and disappearing into the fourth floor. "We ran out of water hose, connected up all we found around here but it only reaches up to there. So . . ." Jojo told how the oil drums were being filled by hose up on the fourth landing then hauled by lift to the other floors where the watchman was watering the planters with cans; a dogged task.

"Wouldn't have to do it if we had some rain," Louie-Louie said uneasily.

"Aw, he can do it, man," Jojo declared. "That Serendip is really something else. Lou ought to see him up there, going

at it. Every day, man. I mean, he's really into his thing, y'know." He cocked his chin upwards admiringly. "Got it all together, y'know, and like he's seventy-five, right Lou-Lou?" That's what they had found out, the other boy told Willie who shrugged.

Joining the boys, Alma said, "The old guy's worried, I think. About no rain."

"He tell you that?" Jojo asked.

"No," the girl said. "Only he is, I can tell."

Willie stood forgotten as the other boys turned to Alma with expressions of concern. In their enthusiasm and drive to get the steelwork planted they hadn't figured on any threat to the success of their plan. They looked up to where a large hook hung at the end of a crane cable past which they could see old Serendip. A pale spot against the background, he was moving across a ninth floor catwalk towards the lift which now had begun another trip upwards.

Neither Louie-Louie, Jojo nor Alma had noticed that no whistle had sounded before the lift set off. Neither had any of them noticed that Willie was gone.

He remained ducked out of sight until he felt he was well on his way. Then, easing himself up inside the oil drum, Willie grinned, peering over the edge. He saw his friends growing smaller on the ground far below. Ahead, through the mesh of the lift cage, he could see the rooftop of his tenement, the pigeon coop, a scatter of birds lofting lazily in the haze crosstown. In a roof directly across the way he saw Otis' oldest brother practicing karate moves with a friend, circling and

feinting one another back and forth across a spread of ratty mattresses.

The quick stop of the lift caught Willie off balance momentarily. Righting himself, he boosted himself out of the drum. The watchman spotted the boy as he came towards the cage. Taken aback, he watched him step out onto the top floor platform.

"Nice ride," Willie said flipply. The old man nodded, entering the lift to move out the crates of seedlings.

"Need a hand, pop?" the boy said with a sneer.

Mr. Serendipity sniffed uneasily. "Why, that's nice of you . . ." His voice trailed off; he didn't know this one's name and plainly the youth was not volunteering it. "Er, thank you all the same, I can manage. As I've told everyone, I'm sorry, but this is out of bounds up here—much too dangerous."

"Yeah?" Willie took in the scene about them with a sweeping glance. "Well, you didn't tell me, man. Anyways, I didn't mean helping you with all this jive you got everybody into." They looked at each other for a long moment.

"Nice ride," Willie said once more. "Look, man, we could get something going here you and me—with this elevator— like, it's so available, right?"

Combined with his initial surprise at Willie's sudden appearance, the boy's rapid words left the old man at a loss. "Available . . ." he said in his absent way when baffled.

"Right, pop. Dig. I'll handle the rides—run the cats up and down—say like for a nickel a ride, maybe three for a dime, something like that, y'know?" Willie looked at the lift and nodded to himself. "Be cool, and like we could divvy up at

the end of every day. No sweat, pop. Real easy bread. You just show me the ins and outs of the thing. Seems nothing to it—I got it up here myself." Willie laughed. "So we could pick us up some nice change, see? Hey, you listening, pop?"

The watchman removed two crates of seedlings and placed them on the platform before replying. "Oh. Well," he said softly. "I'm afraid that's not the sort of, er . . . thing we're doing here."

Willie drew himself up, snickering, "Oh yeah? What *is* it exactly then, you're into?"

"This is just something to enjoy," the watchman said. "We're growing some things. I guess that's about it, son. Growing a few things. Here is this lot; all of it just lying around, mouldering, don't you know? And . . ." He waved skyward. "There's the sun. It's all free—as you say, available."

The boy eyed him icily. "Sure. Till the catch."

"The . . . catch?"

"The catch, the kicker, the trick-bag, man. C'mon you don't get nothing f'nothing. This another of them poverty pro-gram tricks, pop?"

Old Serendipity threw up his hands, his head wagging in puzzlement. "Sorry," he sighed, "afraid I'm dense about some things." He motioned for Willie to step inside the lift, and rolled the oil drum aside, preparing to descend.

He threw the lever and they rode down to the fourth floor where Willie watched the old man wrestle the drum out and over to a hose line nearby. "We can't risk waiting for rain any longer," he told the boy as he turned on the nozzle, hanging the hose into the drum. Mr. Serendipity shaded his eyes and

peered at the sky unhappily. Willie made a scoffing sound and left the cage.

"Better than watching for clouds, man, you keep an eye on my birds over there. Yeah, those up there," he said. "See 'em?"

"That fine flock? *Your* birds?"

"Mine and my brother's," he said fiercely. "Used to be my old man took care of them but he gets tired, so we run 'em. Anyways, when you see the birds like flying close in circles, small circles around and around, sticking close to the coop—especially in the mornings . . ."

"Yes?"

"Means it's going to rain."

"Really?"

Willie looked across at a long line of seedlings. "Beats them jokers with their weather satellites on TV lots of times. All them radar reports—nothing, man, next to pigeons."

Openly admiring of the boy's knowledge of birds, the watchman asked Willie to tell him more.

"Nah," the boy corrected him. "I only know about pigeons, plain street pigeons which is all they are. But smart though, real cool birds. Most people think they're just dirty birds—and they are. Live in dirt, eat dirt." He laughed proudly. "Yeah, just a bunch of dirty street birds, man."

"Yes, come to think of it," the watchman said, "I've seen you up there feeding them."

"Eat dirt. A few minutes after you fill up their trays they're covered with dirt. I think that's why they such great flyers, maybe. Yeah." Willie watched the flock swoop across the horizon. "I really dig those dirty birds, man."

The watchman caught the note of deep pride in Willie's words. He patted a handkerchief about his neck and asked Willie if he would reconsider and join his friends at gardening.

"Not a chance," Willie said. "Uh uh, not my thing, man. No way."

"Ah well," Mr. Serendipity said. "Perhaps then you'll keep an eye on your flock for us and put in a good word with them. We sure can use some rain, and very soon."

Willie shifted in place. "Oughta get one of the guys to put in a word for you with Aunt Roselita. Yeah, she could be your best bet. Only cost you maybe three bucks, including the goober dust and all."

Throwing the lift lever, they began to take the oil drum up to the top floor in silence. Willie laughed softly to himself, saying, "Yeah, come to think of it, man, you and her would get along . . . like, she's almost as weird as you."

·WAITING·

The lot had become their special place even before they had begun to plant the steelwork. And, by the time the neighborhood kids had helped set the last seedling into place on the top floor, it had become their own, their private world. The other one, the one outside the tall ring of fence, belonged to grown-ups. No one had to tell them that the hip thing to do to keep matters this way was to cool it. This was as street-wise and shrewd a crew as any around the city.

As events had it, keeping their secret was easy.

With the construction strike a solid success, the pickets no longer had to come and patrol the boardwalk. Now and then a union agent stopped by to see that no work was going on,

then left, completely uninterested in the scatter of kids he may have noticed fooling around on the site. As for parents along West 21ST, they were pleased—their offspring were occupied and out of their hair during those long summer days.

There had been enough flower seedlings to line the south face of one wing of the steelwork. At Alma's suggestion, the old man had gone and bought several blooming climbers. Already in full bud, these were planted in some of the empty nail kegs strewn about the lot and lifted to the upper stories of the steelwork, then placed wherever they might look to best advantage along the catwalks.

When a pair of potted vine geraniums were hung from the hooks at the end of the cable cranes over the unfinished staircases, Alma called, "Oh wow! The icing on the cake." A cheer went up all around. It was done; their tower had been planted.

"We, um, just wait now . . . huh?" Doreen asked. She twisted about in the cab seat of the bulldozer, looking to Alma who sat lost in the sight of the vine-geraniums looming high above.

"Huh?" the four-year-old whined when there was no reply. Why was it no one ever seemed to listen to her? She tugged her big sister's sleeve.

"Wha—?" Alma mumbled, lips barely moving.

Doreen slapped the dashboard in frustration, slumping down in the seat, one thin brown leg swinging furiously.

"It'll be something, Doreen," Mr. Serendipity was heard to say. Peering downward the little girl saw the watchman

nearby, Ag at his side. "You'll see," he added, aiming a pointed smile right at Agamemnon.

Doreen slid up in her seat. "That's good," she said after the old man who went shuffling off. "It better 'cause we worked awful hard!"

While passing along a line of seedlings up on the sixth floor one night, trailing water from a can, Mr. Serendipity heard a knocking come from far below. When it came again, louder, he traced it across to the gate. He hurried to the lift, noticing it was after eleven on his time clock.

Hastening across the lot, a lantern in his hand, he heard, "Hey, c'mon man, open up!" He reached the gate as the pounding grew louder.

"C'mon man, we don't have all night—it's me, Willie!"

The old man swung open the gate, raising his lantern.

It was Willie sure enough—a swift cocky grin out of the street darkness, sleeves rolled up into high pretzels, tiny saint's medal a pinpoint of silver from his open shirt. There was someone with him. Old Serendipity smelled a scent of spices, ginger, or perhaps cinnamon. He heard the rustle of long skirts and the clicking of many strands of beads. A woman stepped into the light.

Tall and gaunt-faced, she jutted her jaw twice towards the old man, asking Willie something about him, her long earrings tinkling.

"Right, this is the guy," Willie replied flatly, repeating his words in Spanish to the woman as she listened attentively to him.

Her tawny face became a frown as she looked the watchman over, one eyelid drooped and fluttered oddly, the gumdrop she was sucking showing for an instant between a gap in her front teeth. The old man glanced at a tear in the multicolored brocade skirt which swayed unevenly an inch above her ankles. Willie led the woman through onto the lot, the watchman walking alongside them.

"Aunt Roselita," Willie shot back at him. "She's Dominican —not really my aunt y'know, just everybody calls her that." The boy paused, the woman walking ahead. "You can rap with her, only she don't speak English. That's what people do, rap with her, I mean about problems," Willie sniffed. "Lou-Lou and the guys—they're so uptight about no rain. So I told her, like . . ."

He shrugged and catching up to Aunt Roselita said something to her in rapid Spanish.

In a manner both courtly and shy, the watchman welcomed his guest, Willie translating.

"Perhaps she would like a cup of tea," the watchman suggested cheerily. "I have some fresh danish and the tea is truly fine, it's jasmine. Do you think?"

"Nah, man," Willie said with a jerk of his thumb. "She don't have time, man; she begins her thing over at her place at midnight. Always a lot of people waiting for her."

They walked on past the shed, the boy translating Mr. Serendipity's words for the woman. Arriving some ten yards before the looming steelwork, Aunt Roselita stopped abruptly. Looking upwards she shut her eyes and brought two ringed fingers up to her forehead. Now her eyes flew open. She made

a moaning sound and quickly dipped a hand deep into the shopping bag she carried.

"Hey," Willie whispered hoarsely to Mr. Serendipity. "You got three bucks, pop? Good. Like that's cheap for her coming to the house. Cash, no credit, pop—excepting for people out of work. You got the three then? Okay."

Old Serendipity nodded, watching the woman sprinkle a fine trail of bright red powder over the ground in a mysterious design. His puzzlement turning to fascination, he heard her intone a strange series of words.

"That's goober dust she's using—the best," Willie informed him. "It costs."

The old man blinked as the woman's voice rose. "Is . . . is she a gypsy?"

"I don't know—I don't think so. Hey, Aunt Roselita," the boy called in Spanish. "You a gypsy? The old guy wants to know."

Willie's question made the woman stop and straighten sharply. A stream of words from her filled the air like a flurry of poisoned darts. The watchman shrank backwards.

"Oh, wow!" whooped Willie, laughing. "Oh, man, can she curse beautiful! You better not say that again, pop. She's no gypsy—nothing like that, can't stand being called that. You shoulda heard what she called you."

"Oh," murmured the old man sheepishly. "Please tell her I'm sorry."

"Forget it. She's a *spiritis* lady."

"Beg your pardon?"

"A spirit lady, Latin-style; a conjure woman, dig? Like her

mother, she said. Used to do her thing in Santo Domingo, only now in her apartment two floors under us." Willie drew himself up. "Me—I don't really believe all of that, but like a lot of people go to her. A lot of problems around, man."

"I see . . . she helps people then."

"Sicknesses mostly," Willie said. "Or if you have a kid born with a twisted-up leg. My old lady goes; she swears by Aunt Roselita. Not my old man though. Puts her down—but maybe he ought to try her for getting rid of his headaches he's always having." Willie pointed at the spirit woman who, with a thin stick, was now drawing a large circle around the pattern of red dust.

"But who knows?" the boy said. "She might get you some rain—only three bucks."

Mr. Serendipity ran a hand over his beard, listening to a mysterious incantation coming from the woman. "We certainly could use some rain badly, son."

Willie scowled. "Okay—only quit calling me son, man." The boy left his side for awhile, saying, "You got nothing to lose—least it's a good show once she really gets into her thing."

He tiptoed back to the watchman's side, lowering his voice. "They say she can put on the Evil Eye."

"The . . . Oh, my."

"Right—the whammy. They say she once put the Eye on some cat way up in the Bronx and zap, halfways across the Triborough Bridge, the motor drops out of his brand new car. Crunch, man."

When the old man looked towards the steelwork again

he didn't see the woman anywhere. Not long after, they heard a shriek from the dark within the construction, then an eerie cry of delight and a babble of shrill words, laced with Agamemnon's bleating. Ag! The watchman gulped and went stumbling towards the steelwork, Willie after him.

The boy, calling out for him not to worry, tripped in a vegetable plot.

Old Serendipity came to a wavering stop at the foot of the steelwork, his lantern revealing Ag splaylegged out at the end of his tether line, his eyes like glistening saucers. Bent in a crouch circling before him, Aunt Roselita was waving a forked hand in the air, another mysterious incantation welling out of her.

"Aaaagg," said the watchman weakly.

"Be cool, man," Willie warned, arriving next to him. "She won't hurt him, but there's no telling what she might do to you, you go messing into her business now. She's really working into it now."

The old man heard the woman utter the word "Diablo . . ." from amidst her wailing, a word he understood. *Devil?* He gulped.

"What . . . sort of . . . way," he stammered, "is this to . . . call for rain?"

The boy shushed him be still. Then cocking his head he listened to the spirit woman's chanting. She had fallen into a trance and now began to light a series of candles in shallow glasses which sat in an arc on the ground before the goat. Their flames flickering, misshapen shadows danced across the nearest orange girders.

"Yeah," Willie said, "it's rain she's working on."

The woman's voice spiraled up into a chilling moan. "But what's this to do with Ag? Why does she say 'the devil'?" the watchman rasped.

The boy grinned. "Says she has to rid this place of him so's it can rain."

"Get rid of? Not . . . Ag?"

"Him, the devil. Hold it—" Willie's hand shot up like a traffic cop's, calling for silence. Then listening intently for some moments, he nodded. "Yeah. She says His evil spirit's inside your goat, or something. Her Spanish is different to begin with, and now she is really rapping weird—but I think the deal is to clean the evil spirits out of this place, wherever, before she can bring the good things you want. Like rain."

Old Serendipity scratched his head. "In my . . . Ag? The devil?"

Calling for Agamemnon's cleansing, Aunt Roselita began to dance in a wild swirl and rustle of skirts, her arms flailing at the night. With her wails rising and Ag bleating, it took some time before Willie became aware that the old man at his side was doubled over in laughter.

"Of course . . . of course," the watchman said several times. "I should have known," he said, tears of joy rolling down his cheeks. "I should have guessed all along—it was the devil in him. That accounts for it." Rocking on his heels, he leveled a wagging finger towards his goat. "Found out—you're found out at last, old friend." Now it was the boy's turn to be baffled.

The spirit woman swooned down to her knees. And after

a few moments, she came slowly out of her trance. She crossed herself then with a nod of satisfaction, got to her feet.

Mr. Serendipity waited while Willie went to her. After huddling briefly with her, Willie returned to the old man. "One helluva hard job she says it was, pop. Look, why don't you be a sport and make it four," he said, holding up four fingers.

"Gladly," the watchman said, handing the money to Aunt Roselita. He was only sorry she could not stay to tea. He was most grateful for her services—even if it brought no rain. He could not imagine a better way to have spent four dollars.

Ag did not find this crack the least bit funny.

·ALRIGHT·

In Reedsboro township that night the humid air was alive with the chittering of crickets.

On the Mackelgum farm a cicada sang mournfully in the lawn willow while lightning bugs glowed in the dark beyond the house. "Ahhh . . ." Mr. Mackelgum let out a contented puff of cigar smoke. Crossing his feet atop the porch railing, he peered at the vague spread of meadow trees sloping downhill towards the north creek.

"How's my beef pot pie sitting with y'all, Papa?" His daughter's voice reached outside from the clatter of dishes in the kitchen behind the frame wall.

"Oh," said C.H. taking his time replying, "not bad, girl, not

bad. Still got you aways to go though to match up to your Mama's." He drew on the cigar giving it a half turn in his fingers.

"Hunh. Alright, okay," his daughter chided. "For that, see if there's any hot breakfast waiting on you at six tomorrow morning—nasty, unappreciative old man."

The pair shared a brief chuckle on both sides of the wall. Placing the cigar in a jar top ashtray, Mr. Mackelgum sat up and bent over the small table next to him, picking up a pencil.

"Kids sleeping good?" he asked, starting to whittle a point with a penknife.

The round, open face of his daughter appeared at the kitchen window a yard down the porch. "They never have no trouble falling asleep after those stories of yours; heard 'em often enough."

The old farmer grunted. "Hunh—is that so? So happens girl, the three of them sat round me hanging on my every word, without a sound. Hunh—why the little one didn't once stick that thumb in her mouth. You try achieving that some-time."

Blowing him a kiss, the young woman withdrew her head inside the house.

"Say, Leona," Mr. Mackelgum called. "Be so kind and provide some nice letter-writing music for your dear old Papa."

He screwed up his eyes in thought and looked down at the blank postcard on the table. Heck, he told himself, why those little ones had listened without a peep to his story, his "recollec-ions". While the three lay sprawled about him on the big

bed, C.H. Mackelgum had told his grandchildren about the time he was forced to leave school at the start of the sixth grade to work alongside his older brothers and sisters out in the fields. Ten hours a day under a "grinning sun" in order to add his two dollars to the family earnings in the coffee can at the end of a week. "It was mean hard work," he had replied to the oldest's question, "still there was others which worked harder 'n us. Yeah . . . the mules."

The strains of gospel music came drifting from the battered table radio inside the parlor. C.H. Mackelgum wet the tip of the pencil in his lips. Writing a friend was a pleasant prospect.

He tightened his grip on the pencil, hunched over the table, and carefully printed:

Dear Hanibul

He paused, his white eyebrows knitting together like the cap of an ocean wave.

It was good gettin your letter yestiday. Those things you and those kids now doin sound better all the time. Plant somethin for me, petunias would do. Man alive! I new you was the exact man for the job! I sure wish I could see it all when she blooms. Yeah— I been busy myself. The crops are lookin good. I put cabbage and rhubarb in that land in the lowers I told you about.

Mr. Mackelgum stopped writing to flex his stiff fingers, listening to the *gallumpfs* of a bullfrog coming up from the creek. He tapped his pencil then wrote a line about his grandchildren, coming to a close with:

Hope you are startin to look round for a perminint place to live. I would if I was you—strike can't go on forever.

Signing his name to the postcard, Mr. Mackelgum lifted the pencil to his chin, a faraway look coming to his face. The insect sounds seemed to be growing louder and a mist was now rolling up from the "lowers".

"Weather seems to be working itself up, Mister Mackelgum." His son-in-law stepped out onto the porch, a floorboard groaning. A stockily-built young man in overalls, he nodded. "Best to be coming in, don't you think?"

Mr. Mackelgum snorted indifferently, asking, "How's the pickup—you get the new battery hooked up?"

His son-in-law made a clucking sound. "Hooked up, the spark plugs cleaned and the motor all tuned. She runs noisy as a well-pump, but if she had to, the old gal could still make a run with a load of 'taters to Mobile."

"And back?" Mr. Mackelgum quickly asked.

"And back, Mister Mackelgum—stake my reputation on it."

"Hmm . . ." The old farmer eyed him thoughtfully. "Gas in the tank?"

"Gauge don't read, but she's near full. Why? You don't happen to be running off with some young gal, are you?"

They both laughed, Mr. Mackelgum saying, "Once was enough—but that's a thought, a thought. No, I was jest thinking to take me a ride, come morning."

The plop and spatter of several large raindrops sounded on the tin roof of the porch. The innocent start of a first-class summer storm, the raindrops soon became a downpour, the

heavens rumbling and opening wide. Sheets of water drenched the lawn, bending the willow tree; rivulets streamed down the north meadow, the creek swamping its banks.

The rain that hit New York that night was not as heavy, the city catching only the edge of the storm sweeping the eastern seaboard. But it was nearly as dramatic to the eye; thunder and the crackle of lightning in the pitch black skies over the sky-scrapers.

There were a lot of anxious youngsters on West 21st who peered uneasily through blinds and past windowshades at the construction down the block. In the lightning flashes the nine stories of steelwork turned fiery orange, the long lines of flowers in the girders becoming wildly tossing ranks of poison-ous-looking yellow-green and turquoise.

Towards dawn, while TV sets sat blind and neighborhood men were returning from night shifts in hospitals and hotel kitchens, the storm blew out to sea. And, when the first pearly light had arrived over Manhattan, it began. High and low, across the southern face of one wing of the nine-story frame of America's finest factory-steel, thousands of buds began opening in the fresh, new sunlight.

·OH, WOW!·

Although there is no way of knowing for sure, in all likelihood it was Willie who saw it first.

As soon as there was light the boy had gone up to the roof to see how the flock had fared in the storm. Entering directly into the coop, he checked over the birds. Some of them were ruffled and quite damp, but otherwise they appeared to be well, strutting and cooing along their shelves. Willie swept out the floor. He pushed a puddle out with the broom, latched the door, then yawned, rubbing a sleeper from his right eye.

Thus, it was only his left eye which spotted it first. When both his eyes focused together on the sight, Willie reeled, so stunned that the image down the block did not immediately

register in his brain as being real. He still felt warm from his bed. Could be, he thought, I'm still asleep. The boy knew he had walked in his sleep sometimes. Hadn't his father twice found him padding down the hall in his pajamas, his hands outstretched like a zombie?

Willie stepped up to the parapet wall and stood there—gaping.

It stood dazzling, glorious in the clean light after the storm. Some one-hundred-and-fifty feet high by sixty feet across, the wing of steelwork danced with flowers, leaf and vine, in a gentle river breeze. In long rows, the blooms were massed in rills, frills and spills; stands and bands of every shape; lines, spines and clusters of every shade of every flowering color.

Among the annuals were double nasturtiums in scarlet, gold and pumpkin. Portulaca, plain and hybrid, competed with petunias and marigolds along the running yards of rusting girders. Delft blue and violet morning glories twisted up ladders and posts from their nail kegs and snaked along cables past pockets of giant daisies and cornflowers. Poking outward from between tie rods and framing into the sun were borders of baby's-breath and bachelor buttons. Climbing honeysuckle laden with pink and white bells clung to wire mesh and curled over abandoned tools and supplies. Here and there on the catwalks stood tubs of tall-stemmed zinnias with blooms the size of softballs, while borders of ice-blue, vermilion and yellow blooms ringed corner I-beams; and high on upper scaffoldings, giant daisies waved over the street.

As the hours passed, there would be more buds continuing to open; those flattened by rain only now beginning to raise

themselves; creepers coming to life. And towering above it all, the tubs of vine geraniums on the crane hooks hung like flower chandeliers, arms of fuschia pink cascading downward on all sides.

It would not be long before the massed aromas of sweetness began to attract bees from the Jersey countryside across the river.

Willie, standing on the parapet wall, had a circle of fingers in his lips trying to get a whistle out without much luck. When finally he did, the signal brought Jojo sleepily out the window below and onto the fire escape. He looked up to see Willie gesturing and yelling like a madman. One look across the street sent Jojo leaping back into the room and scrambling for his clothes. Tangled in the arm of a shirt, he raced past his uncle's bed, the man staring dumbfounded after him.

Willie vaulted a wall onto the next roof and bounded for the fire escape at the rear. Barely skimming the slat-iron steps, he arrived at Otis' window and tapped on the pane with his skull ring. The older boy blinked blearily out of sleep, then, when the news shouted at him sank in, sat bolt upright throwing off covers. Otis went stumbling out into the hallway and over to the dumb-waiter where he called down the shaft to Chico and Chino, three floors below.

Mr. Serendipity's alarm still had three hours to go before ringing. The old man snored heavily until Ag managed to awaken him by licking his ear.

"My, my," the watchman said with a fuzzy smile, ignorant of what was outside. He worked his empty gums. "So nice,

wasn't it, being lulled to sleep by that rain?" Rain . . . ? The thought struck him. "Do you—do you suppose Aunt Rose-lita . . . ?"

He fished his teeth out of a cup on the bedside table. "Wasn't the lady *some*thing, Ag? My!" The old man stood and laughed, forking the fingers of one hand and passing them in the air over the goat's head in mimic of the spirit woman. Ag turned sourly and clomped off.

The watchman went to the wash basin. "Seems to me a nice shave is in order today. Mmm." He drew a deep breath. "Just smell that fresh after-a-rain air."

He worked up a thick lather on his face and leaned in, his razor poised to begin. Reflected in the cracked mirror, through the open window behind him, he saw it—promptly nicking his chin.

Old Serendipity rushed to the door, the sun catching him full in the face as he flung it open. All he could think was that it was unbelievable, yet, somehow, *just* the way he had imagined it would be. The belt of his bathrobe trailing, shaving lather dripping, he ran out on the porch, down the steps and onto the lot. Wordlessly, his eyes ran up and across the flowering steelwork several times. Even Ag appeared to be impressed.

Not bad.

"Not bad?" old Serendipity said, his heart thumping with elation. "Not bad? Why it's as beautiful as I had hoped it'd be and much more than I ever dreamed."

Alma was filling Doreen's bowl with cereal and sipping her juice with the other hand when she saw it out the kitchen

window. Spurting orange when she coughed, the girl lunged from her seat in a cloud of cereal flakes and went racing for the street.

Pell-mell they all came . . . down stairs and fire escapes, up from basements, cutting through alleyways—Pequita, Hands, Louie-Louie, Lucky, Malcolm, Jojo plus a number of assorted cousins, kid brothers and friends. They converged on the main gate from all corners of the block. The old man, wearing his blue serge suit and white shirt, the nick from shaving a bright red spot on his chin, greeted them.

Once inside the lot, a hush fell over the kids as they circled before the steelwork, their heads craned back far as they could go. No one spoke for some time as everyone just looked, their eyes glowing; pounding and poking one another in exchanges of disbelief.

"Well," Mr. Serendipity said at last, clearing his throat. "What do you think of it?"

Shoulders jiggled sheepishly. The kids who were never at a loss for words were suddenly tongue-tied, everyone waiting for someone else to speak first.

"Oh, wow!" Willie said, breaking the silence. "I mean, like for a weird guy, man, you're something else."

"Way outasight, Mister Serendip," Pequita sang.

"Way, way!" someone added.

"Dynamite!" Otis whooped.

Shouts and yells filled the air, the group beginning to dance around the old man, to the tune of Malcolm's transistor; a mix of Indian rain dance, bugaloo and shingaling, until they sagged out of breath.

THE WORLD'S BIGGEST WIERDO lives HERE!!!

This was a Sunday. And in the neighborhood people sleep late after a big Saturday night. They would not see it until about eleven when they filed down the block on the way to church.

The old man asked Hands and another boy to go to the store and buy enough sodas to go around. Then, unable to resist the kids' urging, he agreed to ride everyone up the steel-work in the lift for a close look.

"It's yours," he said, "after all."

Otis grinned. "Yeah—but our *what?*"

"Don't mind him, Mister S," Alma hooted. "You ought to be used to his dumb questions by now."

Alma ducked out of the way as Otis sent a jab at her shoulder.

"But like . . . *why* did you do it?" Jojo asked.

Willie guffawed. "Ah man, talk of dumb questions . . ."

Mr. Serendipity dipped his head, then peering up at the flowers for a moment, said, "No reason, really. It just seemed to ask to be done. Isn't it grand?"

"Just did it to *do* it," Louie-Louie said. "Right?"

Heads nodded.

"Right," Willie summed up. "You don't ask why birds fly —they just fly."

His pals looked at Willie, Lucky reminding him that it was *their* thing he was talking about, "but that's okay, Willie-man, we'll let you look."

Doreen went up to the watchman as the sodas arrived. "It's

like you said it would be," she said with a grin.

Mr. Serendipity spent the next hour taking the groups up to the top floor in the lift, carrying three at a time with him. While Pequita and a classmate of hers stood waiting for their turn, the other girl frowned. "What," she said, "if this gets you in trouble?"

"In trouble?" Pequita replied. "What—for flowers?"

The work-lift came for them. And soon they were being hoisted slowly upwards, oohing and aahing and calling out the flowers' names they passed at each floor.

The lift neared the top floor, the old man proudly saying, "Now those over there are the hybrid nasturiums. Remember we talked about them? If you'll compare them with the plain kind, you'll see—"

Hands cut him off with a soft whistle. "That down there, I think," he said, pointing at the lot far below, "looks like a cop —the plain, ordinary kind."

·OUTSIDERS·

He raised a ballpoint pen over the black notebook in his hand, saying, "So now—you're the one's in charge you say?" The patrolman looked from Mr. Serendipity up at the steelwork for the fifth time, unable to keep his eyes off it.

Old Serendipity beamed. "Oh, yessir, I'm the watchman here and these," he said cheerily, "are my friends. Are you sure you wouldn't care for a cup of tea, perhaps a soda?"

The patrolman's insignia read 74th Precinct, the local station house only blocks away, but none of the kids recognized him; he was a new rookie. The kids huddled closer about the two men, their faces guarded and watchful.

"The watchie," the patrolman said, writing. "Okay—*name?*"

"Why yes, of course," Mr. Serendipity politely replied. "Hannibal Serendipity—middle initial, S." There was a low ripple of giggles from the group. "That's for Ser-va-tius: s . . . e . . . r . . ." The old man stopped spelling, seeing the cop turn to face two other policemen coming towards them now; one a lieutenant and the other a plainclothes detective.

The newcomers approached from between two garden plots, their eyes scanning everything with unconcealed amazement.

"What's coming off here, Brozowski?" the lieutenant called before coming to a stop at the group. The plainclothesman, a dour-faced man with pale eyes, hung back sizing up the group.

"That's sure the question, lieutenant," Patrolman Brozowski said. He tipped his cap up, running the back of his wrist across his damp forehead. "I been trying to ascertain the facts from these people here for fifteen minutes, sir."

The lieutenant drew a squinting bead on the old man. "You know about all this, pop?"

"This guy's the watchie," the patrolman filled in.

"Ah—then he'd know," the plainclothesman said as if he had discovered a vital clue.

Willie nudged Mr. Serendipity, whispering, "Be cool, now."

The patrolman gestured about at the kids. "He stated they did it—that what you said?"

"Oh, yessir," Mr. Serendipity volunteered. "Isn't it *some-thing*, sir? They deserve all the credit."

"We worked hard," peeped Doreen.

"They did all this?" the lieutenant snapped, turning, the brass buttons of his jacket flashing in the sunlight.

The plainclothesman sniffed sourly. "Trying to shove it all on them, looks like. Figures."

Mr. Serendipity was taken aback. "Shove it . . . on . . . I don't understand, sir."

The lieutenant motioned Patrolman Brozowski to step aside with him. They conferred. "What ordinance you booking him on?" the ranking officer asked.

The patrolman hemmed and hawed a moment, withdrawing a thick manual of city codes and ordinances. "That should be easy, but . . ."

"This is private property, right?"

"Check," Brozowski said. "Been shut down since May, sir."

"So we've got a Defacement matter, then."

"Check. Only, when you think about it . . . maybe a Vandalism citation, huh?"

"Hm."

"I could check under Gardening, Illegal Procedures," the patrolman hastened to suggest, flipping pages of the code manual.

"Look, just write it out," the lieutenant said with an impatient wave. "We don't need to make a federal case out of this." The officer walked back to the group. "Tell me, pop, just what is it you had in mind with all this?"

"In mind?" Mr. Serendipity queried. "Why—a garden, sir." It's so simple to see, he thought. Why were these men so upset? He pulled out his handkerchief and wiped a cheek.

"You leave him alone!" Doreen squealed. She stepped out of the group and up to the lieutenant. "He didn't hurt nothing!"

"Like it's only flowers," Pequita said.

"Right," Alma crooned. "And ain't they pretty?"

"Dig," Otis added.

"Are there laws against flowers, too?" Louie-Louie flipped.

"And," Willie said, trying to fight off a grin, "doing things like this keeps us poor kids off the streets—from turning into hood . . . lums. Right?"

"And rioters," Hands said with a pokerface.

"Dig," added Otis.

The three lawmen made some noises among themselves.

"Please," Doreen said. "Leave him alone; he's nice. And so's his goat." The four-year-old grinned with delight at Agamemnon who came ambling from behind a truck.

"Hey!" the detective declared. "That's a goat there."

"Dig."

By noon a growing crowd had collected on the sidewalk opposite the construction fence on West 21st Street. It wasn't long before the police had to put up barriers to make a path for the newsmen and photographers who were now arriving in numbers. Neighborhood people buzzing together in clumps were being joined by passers-by and the usual curiosity-seekers who had heard the news.

Rushing over from the church across Ninth came the priest to find out why there were so many empty pews at Mass that morning. Parishioners who saw him pointed up at the steelwork asking him how he accounted for such a thing. The elderly priest could only wag his head, staring upwards along with everyone else, in his mind fast reviewing all of the miracles and Biblical prophecies he was familiar with. And

across the street in a doorway stood Aunt Roselita making strange signs with her bejeweled fingers and intoning phrases.

By three in the afternoon, with the arrival of television camera crews and the news already on radio, West 21st had to be closed off to traffic between Ninth and Tenth Avenues. *Cuchifrito* and scraped-ice vendors now had free run of the roadway with their carts, their wares selling as fast as they could serve them. Tinny transistor rhythms came from all over; several bands of students who had come from the university downtown stood about clapping to the beat of bongos. Dogs yelped as they scurried about through the clots of milling spectators. There hadn't been such festivities here since the big block-party three years before.

Now threading his way along the crowded sidewalk, the blindman, High John, sought someone to tell him what was going on. When a resident described what everybody was marveling at, High John blinked his unseeing eyes then broke out into gleeful laughter.

Patrolman Brozowski hurried across the lines of TV cables which lay snaking underfoot, and reached the lieutenant.

"Pardon, sir," he said smartly, interrupting the officer's conversation with two newsmen. He waved his black book of city codes and ordinances. "Think I've got it now, sir; just thought I'd check with you."

The lieutenant turned with a look of annoyance. "Got what?"

"The charges, the right ones, sir." The patrolman began quoting from the book. "Now the goat—he's taken care of

under Six-Oh-Eight-Four: Unlicensed Animals et cetera. Okay. Now, the main charge would be ordinance Seven-Three-Three-Nine-Zero: Creating Dangerous Public Spectacle and Nuisance to Persons and Vehicular Traffic." He paused in his recital of charges. "Of course we could tack on Vandalism and Defacement . . . "

"Just write it out," the lieutenant snapped, his face turning red. Growling an oath, he wheeled and went off, the newsmen on his heels, chuckling.

"*Defacement,* Lieutenant?" one of the reporters asked as they went. "*Vandalism?* For flowers?"

The first of several very troubled parents arrived on the lot, pushing through the knots of policemen and press people. On reaching the shed, one mother paused, seeing the old man standing before a battery of cameras and microphones, surrounded by the youngsters. One of several newscaster and TV reporters was asking Mr. Serendipity another in a long string of questions when the worried woman dove forward and, grabbing Alma and Doreen by the wrists, yanked them out of the group.

Doreen barely had time to cast a wave and farewell grin back at the old man before she disappeared.

"*Both* of you messed up in this?" their mother hissed, dragging them towards the main gate.

"But . . . Maaaa . . . Ma . . . listen." Alma pleaded.

"Just y'all wait till your Papa hears about this," the woman said, deaf to her daughters' protests.

The next harried parent that showed up to claim her son was not so gentle.

Otis, Jojo, Louie-Louie and Pequita were soon the only kids left—along with Willie, who stood holding Agamemnon's tether and making faces into the camera. The interview went on, the kids fidgeting and clowning from time to time when the questions shot at them became dull, or worse, sounded dumb. Mr. Serendipity's mouth felt dry, his feet ached, and his eyes began to burn, but he answered each question, polite as always.

"So," a newscaster asked, shoving a hand mike under his nose, "it was after, as you said, you 'set up housekeeping' in this shed, that you started the garden?"

"Not long after." Old Serendipity winced momentarily, flashguns going off, shutters clicking in the background. "There was nothing here for me to do in the daytime."

"Do we take it then," another man said, thrusting himself forward, "that this is, ah, your first . . . creation of this sort?"

Mr. Serendipity smiled at his young friends. "The first for any of us. I've raised window plants before, geraniums mostly."

"Yes. Well," the newscaster said quickly, "are you aware that in modern art today what you, ah, have done here might be called a form of environmental sculpture? A restructuring of reality for no purpose other than the visual experience?"

The old man's face became blank. "How's that again?"

"Then your intention was not along the line of some kind of avant-garde art here?" a third reporter asked.

"Hey you guys for *real?*" Willie jeered.

"Avant-garde art, sonny," the reporter explained, as if he were talking to a third grader. "Heh, heh . . . far-out modern art." He patted Willie on the head, turning to look at the

cameras and the unseen TV audience. "This lad is Willie Martinez, folks, one of the neighbor—"

"Hi, Ma! Hi, Pa!" Willie broke in, waving at the cameras. "Hey, Ramon—we doing our best!" Then turning serious, the boy said, "Aw, man, c'mon with that—they didn't guard any, whatever you said." He waved about in a sweeping arc. "Just look around man, you can *see* what it's all about."

"That's all it takes, man, looking," Otis snickered. He turned to Jojo. "What's with these cats? Ain't they got *eyes?*"

"Now can the old man go, mister?" Pequita said, looking with concern at the watchman. "He's tired. Besides, if you can't understand what it's about, then, like nothing we can say is gonna help you."

The combined decision of the police, construction company officials and two men from the mayor's office was not to file charges against the watchman or the kids.

However, an emergency crew of workmen that had been summoned to the work site went up into the girders of the south wing of the steelwork. And, as Pequita took the old man's hand, and the small group walked away from the cameras, the first clump of flowers were ripped up and came hurtling down through space. Soon, vines and plants by the shovelful followed, plummeting downward, soil and leaves scattering, uprooted flowers striking the ground with dull thuds.

"Shame! Shame! Shame!" Cries and boos began to go up from the young onlookers beyond the fence.

On the pavement outside, long-haired students started marching and shouting, "Save the flower tower! Save the

flower tower!" until this became a loud steady chant from many throats. Still, flowers kept falling from the steelwork, and tears filled the eyes of some girls.

The executive vice president of the construction company, having arrived from his summer home, went into a hasty conference with police and city officials. The shouts from outside the fence growing angrier. Turning to his assistant, the man snapped, "This is bad—the publicity will ruin us. How do we look on TV, tearing up flowers? Have it stopped immediately. And bring that old kook and the kids over so they can get some pictures of me with them."

The man's order was quickly passed up to the workmen. The rain of flowers was stopped and cheers arose from the street. When High John heard what the cheering was all about he yelled for joy. Moving out into the street, the blindman started clapping and singing while around him a circle of young people who danced in their bare feet was forming.

Patrolman Brozowski joined those who went looking around the lot for Mr. Serendipity, but neither the old man, the kids, nor Agamemnon could be found anywhere.

.THEIRS.

Willie walked ahead, leading Ag. The others trailed behind, walking glumly through the weed-covered vacant lot where Lucky had once made his fabulous find amongst the trash. Hanging like a pall over them was their last image of uprooted plants falling to the ground.

Mr. Serendipity paused, lighting his pipe. "My," he said. "Must be past five; it's been a long day." He took a seat on a wooden crate in the tall grass-weed, his eyes on Agamemnon munching something. "Cheer up," the old man said without much gusto. "You said yourself, remember—the important thing was doing it. No one can take that away from us."

Nobody replied. Otis and Louie-Louie tossed stones at

empty bottles and cans and Willie jammed his hands deeper into his dungarees.

"We don't feel bad for us, Mister Serendipity," Pequita said. "Uh, uh—for you."

The old man looked up in surprise. "For me? Now, isn't that something? Here I was feeling awful for all of you."

A crumpled beer can hopped from the grass, one of the boys' stones having hit its target. "At least," Otis said slowly, "we got us places to sleep—they ain't much, but at least places."

"Ahh," Mr. Serendipity sighed. "I see. Well, it was that first move after all those years that was the jolt for me and Ag. But we got through that all right." He brightened, shaking his head. "And things turned out." He winked across at Ag. "They sure did. A whole lot better than we expected, eh, old friend? Yes, we'll manage—something will turn up."

Speak for yourself, old man.

Old Serendipity grinned. "Sorry, Ag, I'm speaking for both of us. Like it or not, that's the way it has to be from here on. You're the goat—and I'm the man, such as I am. Time we got a few things straight between us. So . . . just leave things to me, Ag."

To you?! Leave things to—

"Cor-rect, old friend. Unless, that is, you're prepared to go off on your own."

Agamemnon broke off staring at the watchman and backed away. The kids stood taking this all in, their eyes narrowed suspiciously to slits, moving back and forth from man to animal. "Nice guy or not," Lucky whispered to Otis, "that cat is totally freaked, man."

Finding their eyes on him, the old man laughed. "Oh yes," he said, guessing the question in their minds. "He and I have our chats from time to time."

"Hm," Pequita murmured, embarrassed for him. "But Ag— I mean—he don't say anything back. Does he?"

"Nope, he doesn't."

The kids exchanged wary looks.

"But," Mr. Serendipity added, "does he ever talk back! In his own way, that is. These Serbian goats are a cantankerous breed."

"Say," Willie suggested, fast changing the subject, "there's something over at Lou-Lou's place you oughta see."

Hands offered to stay with Ag in the empty lot while the others took Mr. Serendipity to Louie-Louie's, a tenement over on Ninth. They walked by way of 23rd Street, a broad thoroughfare, this section lined with printing firms, cheap appliance and clothing stores which were closed for the day.

In passing a shop, Pequita veered off to look at a color TV set which played soundlessly inside the display window. "Look —*mira*—look!" she suddenly cried. "*Mira!* It's us— there on the TV! On the Six O'Clock News!"

Everyone charged to the shop window and pressed up against it. Oh wow! Yeah, it was! "Us!"

Otis jabbed the old man in excitement. "Whooo-wee, pops! Look—there's you . . . and Jojo and . . . there's *me!* Me, man! See me behind Ag there!"

"Yeah. Hey, where's *me?*" Willie shouted. His nose flattened against the glass as he searched for his image on the glowing

tube. "Oh, yeah! there. Look at the jerk patting me on the head like a baby."

"That's the part," Jojo crowed, "where those cats were jiving us with them fancy-dude words."

The group snickered, leaning close to the glass and trying to catch the words shielded from them by the window. There was Willie calling and waving to his family; the old man under a press of microphones with a foolish look as he answered a question; now a long view of the flowering steelwork; and a close-up of Pequita.

"Ooo!" she sang. "That's where I'm telling we live on the block, and how we go there every day to garden."

"Right—right!" Willie cut in. "Look, Otis is putting them on." The boy mimicked Otis' hoarse voice, saying: "Like we're only a bunch of *poor* kids, you know . . . with only rats to play with."

Everyone dissolved into whooping giggles, Otis holding his sides and tottering from side to side.

"Otis, baby," Jojo laughed. "How you put them clowns on something fierce."

The kids were in high spirits. Taking a shortcut, they cut through an alley behind a bargain store.

"You mean," the old man asked Otis off to a side, "that you really don't have rats in your building? I sure had them on 22nd."

The chubby-faced youth sniffed. "Aw, man, of course we do—who don't? Only," he said with a grin, "we sure don't play housie-house with them."

They went up to Louie-Louie's rooftop, taking "their way"—
an in and out trek through the alley, over a low fence, through
a littered backyard, then, by way of the basement, up five
rickety flights to the roof door.

The tar surface, soft from the day's heat, was tacky, making
noises underfoot. Mr. Serendipity followed them between
chimneys of scarred brick, soot-blackened and scrawled with
kids' names. The aromas of a dozen dinners cooking hung in
the sultry air.

"Here," Willie called. "Over this way, Mister Sendendip—
take a look."

Louie-Louie turned away, on the verge of blushing. Pequita
pointed at him. Although he was the oldest boy, he stood self-
consciously, rubbing the ballpoint tattoos on one arm.

"He's bashful," Pequita said. "C'mon, Lou-Lou, show the
man."

Old Serendipity, now emerging from under a clothesline
laden with washing, let out a choked sound of surprise. Before
him lined along the roof, sitting on boards supported by loose
bricks, was a long double line of some fifteen large tin cans and
enamel basins. Each with a plant in full bloom.

"Agh . . . " Louie-Louie mumbled sheepishly, "just some
petunias and crap . . . "

The old man bent low, and passed along over the flowers,
keenly examining them. "My word . . . marigolds . . . and these
geraniums, so fine, and double nasturtiums, too!" He straightened. "You deserve congratulations."

Louie-Louie snuffled and ran a hand through his hair.

"All from seed?" the old man asked him.

"Nah."

"From cutting, then?"

"Nah." Louie-Louie shrugged. "With seedlings I . . . copped from over your place. When we was—y'know."

"Copped?" the old man echoed uncertainly. "*Copped!* Of course, yes, yes," he said with a grin. "Tell me, did you use river silt?"

"Uh huh, like you showed. Plus some stuff Willie here brought over."

"Stuff I sweep out from the pigeons, y'know?" Willie explained. "It works good."

Mr. Serendipity smacked his palms together. "Splendid! An organic garden. Splendid." He gazed about the roof top. "Couldn't have a better place for it here."

"Yeah, it's pretty good—so long's we can keep the alleycats off," Louie-Louie said. "So far the junkies don't bother the flowers none when they come round."

"Ah, yes, those poor fellows." Mr. Serendipity opened his arms wide. "All this space for a garden," he said.

"And next door here," Willie said, hopping onto a parapet wall.

"And there and down the line," Pequita sang; she indicated the four adjoining roofs.

"Cool!" Otis shouted, his imagination stirred. "Why not hang pots from the TV antennas."

Willie laughed and bent to look down over the edge of the roof. "Dig it—some vines—we could start 'em crawling up and down the firescapes!"

"And twisting, working their way across the clotheslines," Jojo called.

"Right!"

"We start some creepers up from Hands' apartment," Jojo added, "connecting up with some from here."

"Yeah!"

"Tough!"

Otis raced across the tar paper. "Man! Flowers climbing all over the alleys . . . "

"And covering all the garbage cans—hoowee!" Willie did a little dance across a ledge.

The street kids went on like this, sharing their visions of what might be until they were out of breath. Looking at them wipe their brows, eyes shining, old Serendipity felt that it all had come to something, after all. What exactly, he wasn't sure of at the moment, but the thought made him feel that it was good And, most important, it was theirs now to carry on.

"Pheww," Otis breathed, sitting down and fanning himself. "Hot, man . . . "

"I suppose," Mr. Serendipity said, just as someone's mother was heard calling. "I suppose I should write the construction people a letter of resignation."

Willie shook his head, grinning. "You for real? Man—you been fired."

The old man caught himself with a laugh; that hadn't occured to him. "Supper time!" they heard. It was Pequita's godmother calling from somewhere below. The kids got up slowly, in no mood to hurry. It was time for good-bye; everyone felt it. Yet now that it was here no one knew how to begin.

"You know," said Mr. Serendipity with a twinkle as they passed Louie-Louie's flowers. "You might try, well . . . saying a few words to them once in awhile. You know, a few quiet words in the cool of the evening? I believe it can help them grow, I do."

They reached the door to the stairway down. "Hey, he really means that," Otis said to the others after checking the old man's expression.

Old Serendipity nodded. "Yes. But then—I'm a loony old kook, aren't I?" he grinned.

Downstairs in the street they paused alongside the stoop for a last round of "so longs" and "take cares". Asking the four to send his good-bye and regards to all the others, he went off accompanied by Willie and Otis.

They walked him to the empty lot where old Serendipity thanked Hands for looking after Ag. Some twenty minutes later, the boys left.

"See you around . . . " they called.

· SEEDS ·

*Okay, old man. Since you seem to be running everything now
—where huh, do we sleep?*

Mr. Serendipity's only reply was a bemused little tilt of his
head. Turning, he gazed again at the swiftly moving river. A
trio of seagulls overhead continued their shrill argument, wheel-
ing about in the warm breeze. From his seat on the pier the old
man watched one dive and spear up some morsel from the oil-
slicked waters, its companions giving chase.

Here the two of them were, he thought, homeless again. But,
odd—he hadn't the least feeling of worry. To the contrary, he
felt a quiet sort of satisfaction and a new, almost heady loose-
ness. Mr. Serendipity nodded to himself, tapped out his pipe
and refilled it.

Ag, sniffing along the edge of the pier at the line of ice cream wrappers and other bits of litter, stopped and came clomping back to stand stiffly before him.

So?

"I must admit," the old man said, taking his time, "that where we sleep tonight is about the last thing on my mind right now. No. *The* last." He looked about them, gesturing. "Look at it, old friend, look. Why there's a whole world out here. Look— see it? Doesn't it make you feel young again?"

Ag looked far from impressed. He may well have been re- calling another day along the river, at a place about a mile downtown when, as a frail kid, years before, he had slipped out of a cattle car and wandered lost and miserable in a driving rain, until the old man happened across him along the railroad siding.

"Why," Mr. Serendipity declared, "with the weather this way we could sleep under that bridge up river, or in some park —that might be fun. Lots of places better than a dank, musty cellar."

The backfire which came from a car moving under the elevated highway beyond, sent the goat skidding for cover. Old Serendipity paid it no mind, then noticed the car heading in their direction, now slowing on the gravel parking area some ten yards ahead. From what he could make out in the failing light, it was a battered pickup truck, small, with an open slat- sided back.

It rolled to a stop, its muddy fenders bouncing noisily as it was shaken by another backfire. The motor was cut off. Steam came hissing from its radiator and from behind the steam, a

voice: "Looks a sight, don't she? Yeah, scared some of those other drivers, but she got me here."

There was no mistaking the raspy laughing tones, though the short figure that came towards him took a moment longer to make out.

"Alright alright . . . Really got yourself into something back there, didn't you? Hoowee . . . saw it all, man. Nine floors of old Hann . . . ibul's glory. All right!"

With a look of disbelief, Mr. Serendipity went and threw his arms around the man. And for some time the two old men stood thumping each other about the shoulders and tossing questions back and forth without waiting for complete answers.

Mr. Mackelgum said he had driven directly to the construction site upon arriving in the city, and was told the whole story by "some street kids who said they was friends of yours." He waved into the air. "I saw it *all*, man."

"You . . . saw it?" Mr. Serendipity stammered. "But how could, I mean—they were tearing it *down*."

"Yeah, they *were*. Heard about it over the radio." Mr. Mackelgum had just reached the Jersey Turnpike when he got the news. "There I was, chugging along nice as could be— when all of a sudden the man's broadcasting all about you— *you* y'ol' fool!"

There was still a police car or two on the scene when he drove up, he went on to tell. Then he ran into a blindman who related how angry people had gotten, shouting for the officials to stop tearing the flowers down. "They didn't *dare* bust it up. You just don't go messing with children and ol' folks! Not

when the television is around to see. When I got there, there was these big floodlights set up, lighting it all up like a moon shot at Cape Kennedy."

They strolled the edge of the pier, Mr. Serendipity wagging his head. "Certainly a funny world, C.H."

Mr. Mackelgum smiled quickly. "You just beginning to discover that, eh? Well, it's more than that, man." He indicated the dark landscape of city buildings spread beyond. "There's a whole lot of troubles out there. Say—c'mon, I'll give you a little ride."

Leading him over to the pickup, he told Mr. Serendipity it was a '53 model, but not to be "discommoded" about riding in it. It had carried him a long way that day. "And I got a personal guarantee from my daughter's husband, it'll get me back, and then some."

"Hey," Mr. Mackelgum said as they got into the cab section. "Somebody you forgetting?"

There was. It took both of them to coax Agamemnon out of the shadows of a building nearby and up into the back of the truck. With the tailgate chained into place, they drove off, the pickup coughing and shuddering until it turned onto a cobblestone road under the raised highway.

Mr. Serendipity sat watching the passing scene for a few moments, a line of freighters now going by.

"Rain hard up this way, too?" Mr. Mackelgum asked.

"Yes, mightily."

".Yeah. Just what people in our line of business needs, eh?"

Mr. Serendipity nodded and turning, waved back at Ag through the rear window.

"How's that friend of yours been?"

"Ag? Oh . . . " Mr. Serendipity chuckled. "Much better. I mean, since he's had the devil taken out of him."

The two men had a good laugh after Mr. Serendipity told the story of the night visit of Aunt Roselita.

"Say, where are you heading, C.H.?"

"No place in particular. Why, you got anything better to do right now?"

"Er, why no."

"Hmm. I didn't think so."

"But, you know?" Mr. Serendipity said, leaning back. "That's of no concern to me, one way or another."

Mr. Mackelgum swiveled his head and looked at him. "It ain't? Well. Sounds like you got yourself together these past couple of months."

"I've never felt better."

"That a fact? How old did you say you is again?"

"Seventy-five."

"Hmm. With no bad habits. Hmm. Listen . . . how's your at-ti-tude, let's say to—"

"Attitude?" Mr. Serendipity broke in.

"At-ti-tude. You wearing cotton in your ears again?"

Mr. Serendipity grimaced. "Heaven forbid."

"Good. I was meaning your attitude towards, well . . . let's say, considering a prop-o-sition. My son-in-law, he's not cut out for farming; been doing it all right, but never had his heart in it. You know young folks these days—he's looking to start him a repair shop in town—loves fixing mechanical things. Which means I could maybe use a partner."

Old Serendipity blinked; he noticed the street lamps now going on around them.

"Partner?" he echoed, not daring to believe his ears.

Mr. Mackelgum made a snuffling sound. "It'll be hard work, lots of it mean sometimes, understand. Sunup to sundown, including Sundays in spring and fall. But a place for your hairy friend, them books of yours. A place."

The stunned expression on his companion's face looked like it would remain forever.

"Well," the dark man said impatiently after a long silence. "If it don't interest you, just say so, man—say so!"

The pickup rattled down a slope in the road and into the gloom of an underpass. When it came out the other end, its occupants were chortling and shaking hands.

"Alright alright," Mr. Mackelgum said. "Got us a deal— yeah, I know me a natural pair of hands for growing things when I see 'em."

Old Serendipity was elated. Twisting around in the seat he tapped on the rear window. "Ag! Did you hear—did you? We're going to . . . to . . ." He turned back. "Where was that again, C.H.?"

"Due south, Hanni . . . bul," Mr. Mackelgum declared. "Two-hundred-seventy miles, give or take. Where there's a field of alfalfa, tell him."

Mr. Mackelgum had to make "a little light run uptown" first; but before he did, they sealed the bargain with a good supper at a diner not far from the riverfront. Then, driving up to a dilapidated row house on 128th Street in Harlem, they picked

up some belongings left behind by Mr. Mackelgum, placing them in the back with Ag, who insisted on knowing *just exactly what's going on, old man?*

It was ten-thirty when the pickup arrived before the main gate of the construction. There it stood, towering in the night sky under the glare of floodlamps, in all its glory.

Mr. Mackelgum hung back on the shed porch letting Mr. Serendipity have the last few moments before departing, to himself. The old man ambled about the steelwork.

"Well, Ag," he said, fingering a squash leaf ."Any thoughts?"

Ag raised his head and sniffed a couple of times.

Not really, old man. As long as there's alfalfa and some nice dirty-faced kids where we're going.

Mr. Serendipity signaled happily that they were ready to leave.

The pickup had limited hauling space. But Mr. Serendipity had no difficulty deciding which of his things to take and which to leave behind. When the tailgate was secured, everything of importance was loaded: some two hundred books, two sickly alarm clocks, a dozen of the best geraniums, and a wicker rocker. And somewhere in the midst of it all, one goat, snoozing away.

Now on the approach to the Lincoln Tunnel toll booth, the pickup waited its turn in a short line of cars. Mr. Serendipity stretched, resettling himself for the long drive ahead.

"You know, C.H." he said, pausing, "Only one thing."

"What's that?"

"I've given it a great deal of thought?"

"Huh? Given what?"

"I'm afraid, well . . . that I have to disagree with you."

Mr. Mackelgum snorted, eyeing his companion sharply. "Will you make sense, man?"

"With all due respect, C.H., I think that your name, that is, that *yours* is really a funnier name than mine."

"Oh, you *do* do you?" Mr. Mackelgum roared, the grin on his face showing his readiness for a good, friendly argument. Thus began the first in a long series of word tussles between Clinton Hezekiah Mackelgum and Hannibal Servatius Serendipity over the years to come.

"Is that so?" Mr. Mackelgum railed as the pickup got onto the Turnpike and headed south. "Let's settle it—let's ask him back there whose *he* thinks is funnier."

Mr. Serendipity laughed; he knew what Ag's answer would be.

Streaks of blue-black and chrome in the moonlight, cars passed them on the highway doing seventy-five and better. The pickup held to the far right lane, swaying under its load at a leisurely thirty-five. But none of its passengers were in any hurry.

The slow pace suited them all fine. There was a great deal to talk over; ideas to consider; plans to be made.

For every second that would pass during the trip from New York to Reedsboro there was a seed waiting to be planted.

ABOUT THE AUTHOR

Herbert Danska has had a highly successful career as graphic artist, illustrator and film-maker. In addition to one-man shows of paintings, he has received numerous awards from the Society of Illustrators, the Art Directors Club, and the American Institute of Graphic Arts.

His film, *The Gift,* which he wrote and directed, won awards at the Venice, Vancouver, and Edinburgh festivals. In addition to many documentaries, he has made two feature films, the newest of which, *Right On!,* is currently on exhibition around the country.

As a children's book illustrator, Mr. Danska has to his credit, among others, *The Selfish Giant, Rory The Red, Queen Without A Crown, Real Book of American Tall Tales* and *Over The Blue Mountain* (for Knopf).

A native New Yorker, Mr. Danska attended the High School of Music and Art, and Pratt Institute here. He is the father of two teenagers, and resides on Manhattan's upper West Side. *The Street Kids* is his first novel.